MIST ON
WATER

SHEA BERKLEY

ISBN-10: 1-942373-04-X
ISBN-13: 978-1-942373-04-9

Published by Thursday Publishing

Cover art and design by Clarissa Yeo

Editing by Robin Perini

To

Robert

MIST ON WATER

CONTENTS

Part Three —— ❖ —— Nari

Long ago in a far off land,
there rose a tale as old as the earth.

As the mist grows heavy,
The father grows tense,
And the mother clutches their babe to her chest.
'Be still, my child; the nix is near.'
The babe hushes,
The mist disappears.
Another day dawns free from the hex.

Before the Descent

Nature wields a powerful force, a power that holds an overwhelming allure, an unstoppable temptation. For some the temptation is in the destructive force of fire—the need to behold the flame as it smolders and burns, to watch it grow and consume until even their own safety is at risk. For others it's the power of a storm—the whip of wind, the lash and sting of rain, and the loud crack of thunder punctuated by a dagger of lightning.

For me, the temptation lay in water. I felt the pull of the hypnotic lap and ebb of the lake outside my parents' house. It projected innocence with the gentle slap and roll of the waves, its fresh scent. Yet sink below its surface and the potential for death awaited with one indrawn breath.

"Ryne," the boom of my father's voice filled the crisp morning.

I tore my gaze from the morning light dancing across the ripple and gurgle of the waterfall. I'd come to this quiet nook, as I had since my fifteenth year, where water met air and earth, where the mist hung thick and moss and fern grew a rich green and the water sparkled like stardust. I was not supposed to be so near the water. For as long as I could remember, my parents told me I must stay away. Evil lurked within its dark depths.

Lately, I'd begun to wonder.

My father had walked far in search of me. I didn't even want to think what would happen if he found me here. I pushed myself from the tree I'd been lazing against and grabbed my bow and arrow before dashing into the forest.

Stealthfully, I made my way through the trees, trailing my father like a hunter would his prey. I stopped short of the clearing where my father had built our house. I could hear my mother's worried voice.

"Did you find him?"

"I told you I would not," the strong timbre of his voice answered. "His bow is missing. He has gone a-hunting."

"Again? He hunts every morn." This was said with slight irritation.

I paused. Between the thick growth of vegetation encircling our home, I gained a position where I was fairly certain to see my parents without being seen. My father, a thick-bodied and handsome man, stood beside my petite and handsome mother. His gaze swept over the forest, touching on my hiding place without recognition before quickly moving on. I released a ragged breath. With one look, I could tell he wondered where I went every morning, but he was not worried.

He turned his attention back to her. "Hunting is a good skill to possess."

She worried her apron as her gaze shimmered

overly bright. "You checked by the lake. He is not there, is he?"

"No, my sweet. He would not go near the lake. He is near full grown. He knows better than that."

Guilt squeezed my heart. My father had so much faith in me. If only he knew…

From my hiding place within the thick brush, I saw my mother's brow wrinkle. "I tell myself that, but I cannot help but think he no longer listens, that the story has become more a bedtime tale than fact."

My father gathered my mother to him, and she laid her head against his chest. He petted her hair with even, calming strokes. "He knows we speak the truth. He knows."

Shame at my deception lashed at me, but it was too late to turn back to the lad I'd been. I turned away and crawled deeper into the forest, my bow now slung across my back alongside a full quiver of arrows.

Truth.

It was a fickle thing. Soren swore that when the moon rose full, mice dressed in trews and shirts and danced before his fireplace.

The truth? Once a month, the pub—full moon or not—brought out a new batch of ale yet to be watered down. My father, along with a handful of stout men, carried Soren home, delirious and babbling, and laid him on the floor before the fire, for his wife would have nothing to do with him when he smelt so badly and kicked at shadows.

Then there was Kilen. His eyes were crossed. Not because he awoke to find a faery perched on his nose three years ago as he claimed, but because he'd had wonky, weak eyes ever since he was a lad.

I would like to say my family was not the type to

dabble in local superstition. But of them all, my family was the worst. And the story they shared since the day I was born was a story of legend as much as it was of ridicule. It defined who I was and who I would be. And I could not shed its affects no matter what I did...for in my parents' eyes I was doomed.

Part One

Ryne

Misfortune comes by night.
Hero or fool,
We all suffer the same.

1

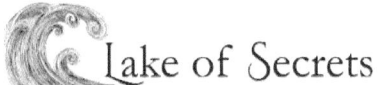 Lake of Secrets

Ghost stories always start out the same—bad blood, bad choices or bad beginnings. Mine encompassed all three. It was told to me that when my parents were young and newly married, my father took all his money and built a house within a stone's throw of the lake. Remote and private, it sat like a pearl above the pebbles lining the shore. People told him it was unwise. What need did a stonemason have with so much water?

"Your house will flood," one helpful friend said.

"Wild animals will overrun your garden," another offered.

True, he risked much so near the cove that would shelter his home. Animal trails littered the ground and flooding was a possibility, but the various reasons his friends gave would not dissuade him, and my father only laughed. "I will hear no more, my good friends. Your advice falls on deaf ears for there is one reason and one alone that steers my labors."

The men waited in anticipation for that reason, and my father gave it willingly. "It pleases my wife to see such beauty."

A groan of understanding rose from the group. "A wife will be a man's downfall if he is not careful," Soren the thatcher replied, a hidden warning ringing within his words.

My father only smiled. "Not *my* wife, or have you not noticed? She is the prettiest, gentlest, sweetest woman God has ever placed on this earth."

No man could say different, for my mother had indeed been the most sought after woman within our corner of the world. That my father, a man of good nature, keen wit, and a ready smile, won her heart made him the luckiest man alive. Surely if any dared fate by building by the lake and prospering–though it was well known prosperity was not in God's plan for our village— my father was that man.

As his friends turned to leave, one tarried. Old man Tiller's face wreathed in worry. "Stay clear of the water. 'Tis cursed."

Old man Tiller was touched in the head, and my father gave the warning little credit. "I am not surprised. Beauty always has a wild side," he said with a laugh. He knew of the ancient curse that had kept men away from the lake, but my father was not a superstitious man.

Tiller would not be put off so easily. "I am serious. There are things unknown, forgotten in time, but I know. I remember. If you are smart, you'll heed my words."

My father's handsome features grew somber, for he did not wish to seem rude. "I have always treated God's creation with utmost reverence. I am not worried."

Old man Tiller eyed my father for a moment and seeing the stubborn streak carved into his character, he shook his head. "Good luck to you then."

"I'll not need any, but thank you all the same," he said, giving the old man's hand a hearty shake.

That was how most of my father's conversations went. He announced his intent, his friends issued warnings and my father proved them wrong. He was a man with an abundance of confidence, and rightly so. Not only was he skilled with stone and chisel, but he could use saw and nail as well as plow and hoe. But the soil was poor and yielded little, and a stonemason's craft is only needed in times of wealth. Our remote village had no claim to money or power. Stubborn as he was, my father would never dream of leaving the place of his birth. So it surprised no one when a few years later, his talents and the lake led him to build a skiff.

The villagers whispered and worried and kept their distance thanks to Old man Tiller and his stories of curses and mysterious sages and unhappily-ever-afters. One drunken word of warning and everyone thought the lake was cursed. Superstition ruled their lives and left them wary. It made no sense to them to court death in a lake no boat in their recollection had ever touched.

All too soon, my father brought my mother to the shore, and to a boat as beautiful as any house he had made.

"What have you here?" my mother said, her hands resting on her gently swelling stomach, a bud of promise, a child desired, but as yet unborn.

My father straightened, the look on his face sober, though hopeful. "Our future."

She patted her abdomen. "Here is our future."

He bent and kissed the swell. His gaze locked onto hers. "A certainty, but this will give us security."

"A boat."

He stood back and waved to the skiff balanced on sturdy piles of wood. "What say you?"

She tilted her head and ran a hand along the bow. The wood gleamed new and perfect in the damp air. "It's almost too pretty to put to water. Are you sure it will float?" she asked, a teasing glint to her eye.

He grabbed her aound the waist, pulling a squeal of delight from her and swatted her bottom playfully. "It will. In fact, so pretty is my boat, the fish will jump in just to admire it up close."

Her eyes shone with love as she brushed a fallen lock from his brow. "Am I to be a fisherman's wife, then?"

"Aye. And a huntsman's, and a stonemason's and a farmer's."

"Next will you learn to weave?"

"Find me a loom, and if it brings me pleasure and profit, I see no harm in it."

She hugged him close. "What did I do that God would bestow such a man on me?"

"Something very good, indeed." He nuzzled her neck and breathed deep of her sweet scent.

She sighed contentedly, for their life held more than the normal thimble of promise. "Indeed."

It took my father no time at all to learn his new trade. Lean and smooth, the skiff glided over the water like a whisper, sneaking up on the fish so that he became almost as masterful a fisherman as he was a stonemason. No harm befell him, and the villagers breathed a sigh of relief. Life was good.

One day, while my father cast and recast his net, a sudden pull nearly jerked the net from his fingers. The skiff dipped dangerously, threatening to overturn. Beads of sweat rose on his skin as he hauled the net closer to the boat. He strained and groaned; his nimble fingers working within the netting to bring the contents closer.

As he worked, the slight wind died, yet the clouds overhead grew thick and angry black. A strange mist curled over the water, surrounding his boat. The eeriness of the moment distracted him, and all of a sudden, pain pierced a finger on his right hand. He gasped, and struggling to keep hold of the net with his left hand, he let go with his right and examined the injury. Blood dripped from his finger, dispersing red rings in the dark water where they grew to ever widening swirls. The beasties in this lake had decided to put up a fight.

Irritated now, he quickly forgot the strangeness of the day, gathered the net in his hands and pulled all the harder. When the bulk of the net thudded against the skiff, he looked down...and into the face of a woman peeking through the netting.

He let go and fell back, landing against the opposite side of the skiff.

Had someone murdered the woman and left her to a watery grave? No. Her skin held a creamy perfection and her gaze had stared straight at him and blinked. As the net skittered out of the boat and flopped open beneath the gentle lap and pull of the water, he wiped the blood from his finger and saw six cleanly imprinted teeth marks on the top and bottom of his finger. No fish made those impressions.

He lunged for the side of the skiff and peered overboard. The water slid glassy smooth all around him, clear turquoise for many feet until the depths darkened to midnight. He stared, probing the water for any movement...and then...a strand of raven black hair floated out from beneath the boat. Delicate fingers slipped along the hull, and then the face came into view.

A beautiful face. Exquisite in every way. A fantasy. A dream. That's what this was. He could only stare, bewitched by the beautiful woman staring back at him.

Without thinking, he reached out his hand. He just wanted to touch her, to find reality in the impossible, but as soon as his fingers slipped beneath the surface, she latched onto his hand and pulled. The sharp tug brought him halfway over the edge of the skiff, but my father was no weakling. Stonemasonry had built thick arms and legs, and a broad, heavily muscled torso. He yanked back, understanding her intent immediately.

A nix. A water sprite. An ancient creature of myth. His mind told him such a creature didn't exist, but his eyes were telling him differently, that he had caught one in his net. He'd dared hunt in her waters and now she wanted revenge—mayhap to make him a slave or feast on his flesh. Those were how the old stories always unfolded. Whatever she wanted, it did not bode well. He had a beloved wife who was heavy with child and a bright future. He would not yield. Yet, no matter how hard he pulled, she would not let go.

Slowly, her dark head crested the water. The mist swirled about her like a living creature. Droplets beaded against her spiked eyelashes and dripped down her skin. Her full, red lips parted and in a singsong voice she said, "It is useless, human, to resist. Come away with me."

Her silent promise spoke to his heart, but his mind stayed firmly focused on his true love. "I will not give in."

His unexpected defiance angered her and the nix dug her nails deep into the skin of his forearm, like talons into a helpless rabbit. He grunted back the pain, but would not yield. He focused on his love and prayed for deliverance. Their tug-of-war recommenced, until my father's shoulder burned and his breath labored. At one point, he managed to pull her against the skiff and snarl into her face, "Rip it from my body, wench, for I will not relinquish the rest."

As the sun broke through the mist and touched the horizon, it briefly highlighted the doubt that entered her honey-colored eyes. She quickly dove beneath the water and pulled harder. After many long moments, the water caressed her skin as she resurfaced. "There is but one way for you to win."

Trust a nix? Did she think him a simpleton? "Your scheming will get you naught," he grunted. Yet, for all his bravado, he was tiring and his arm ached with a deep fire. His whole being was engulfed in the effort to keep himself in the boat. He knew not how much longer he could hold on.

She gave his arm a quick tug as if to gain his attention. "Give me a boon from your cottage, something most precious to you, and I will set you free."

His frown deepened. Most precious? He owned very little of value. What shiny bangle did she mean? "I have nothing you would want."

"It is a risk I will take. Promise me, human…and I shall let you go. But be true, for to promise a nix and then not carry through will curse you forever."

The burn intensified. A groan filled with pain escaped. He saw no clear way of refusal. What cared he if she took a bracelet or his favorite knife or even this skiff, which he prized above all he possessed? He would be free. "Done."

A sudden smile flashed across her face. A jolt of energy surged up his arm and through his body a second before her nails sprang from his forearm, and he fell to the bottom of his boat. He cradled his arm to his side. Pain seared his mind and blood flowed freely. Gulping deeply of the coming night air, he ripped his shirt and bound his arm. This was all a dream. It must be. He had stayed on the lake too long. Exhaustion and lack of water had infected his mind. Yet, when next he looked, his skiff skimmed roughly against the sand and rocks. Somehow, his boat had drifted ashore. He looked behind him and to the water that had grown dark and menacing.

A head rose above the lake. The sun caused a fiery halo to surround the wild hair whipping in the wind. "Remember your promise. I shall come for my boon soon. Amid the mist hovering above the water, I will take it from you."

And with that, she was gone. Almost instantaneously, the sky cleared and the mist receded.

His heart pounded within his chest. He laid back, his skin oddly hot, his vision unfocused. No one would believe him, not even his wife. He lay there for untold minutes. Time rippled past until he gathered enough strength to look toward the house. Its masonry walls gleamed like polished marble in the setting light and seemed miles away instead of only a few yards. Gritting his teeth, he stumbled from the boat and fell to his knees. The world swam before him as he hugged his limp arm to his side. He bent his head to his chest and willed himself to move, but his body would not obey. Light flickered in the window of his cottage, drawing his attention, and again, he gritted his teeth and lunged to his feet. As night extinguished the light of day, a small cry filled the night.

Could it be? Had his wife finally given birth? The sound of joy punctuated the night, mingling with the weak sound of a newborn babe. Son or daughter, he cared not. The small babe would be precious to him no matter what.

Fevered eyes suddenly darted to the water. "No. No,"

he cried and collapsed on the beach, his mind whirling with the weight of his promise. "No," he whispered harshly. "What have I done? God, what have I done?"

2

Unwanted and Rejected

They found my father passed out before the door. The midwife assumed he had drunk himself to sleep after realizing his wife had gone into labor. He did not discourage her from the notion. Better to be thought a drunk than reveal what had just happened to him. But my mother knew something unusual had happened. With one look, she saw his distress. When the midwife put me in his arms, he broke down and sobbed.

The midwife smiled, and whispered to my obviously upset mother. "A natural reaction to finding oneself with a healthy son."

Though my mother smiled and nodded, she was not comforted. She saw the ragged injury to his arm, spied the delirious cast to his eyes and knew trouble had come to their door. My father held me as if I would disappear. I struggled and whimpered until even the midwife noticed and soon rescued me from his desperate embrace. "He'll settle down soon," she said, meaning my father and not me.

Days passed into weeks and the house grew into a routine, one my father did not share. He had yet to settle down as the mid-wife had predicted, leaving well before sun-up and staying away far past nightfall. And whenever the mist rolled in from the lake, his face grew haggard; his footsteps slow. Restlessness ate at his peace of mind, until one night, in the predawn light cast by a heavy moon, he paced the floor. His gaze darting to the water then back at me where I slumbered in my cradle.

The odd tension soon wore my mother raw. She turned over, and found his place in bed empty. Lying quietly, she watched him until her heart grew so sorrowful, she thought it would burst from grief. Propping herself up on an elbow, she called to him. "Why do you pace? Come to bed."

"Do not mind me, my love. I will return shortly."

My mother would not be put off. "No. I cannot ignore your upset a moment longer. Something has happened. Ever since our child was born. I know you were not drunk that night. You were attacked."

His startled look confirmed her fears. "By whom?" she asked. "Who carries such hate that he would try and harm you?"

At first he denied everything, unsure whether he even believed what had happened that night himself, but my mother was not convinced, and my father was unaccustomed to lying. Finally, he sat on the edge of the bed and slumped forward with despair. "I have brought disaster to our family, and I do not know how to fight it."

Unease shone in my mother's eyes. "What has happened? Tell me."

Her growing alarm woke me, and I began to fuss. My mother reached into the cradle they had wedged against the bed and picked me up. She cooed and cuddled, and soon I grew quiet. My father shot me a glance and quickly looked away.

My mother frowned. "You barely look at our son, yet I know you love him."

He winced, but his gaze returned to me. "I try not to. If I can stop loving him, then she will not come."

Silence stretched as my mother fought for understanding. "Who?"

He bent forward, his gaze earnest and a bit frightening to behold. With a hesitant finger, he traced the outline of my tiny lips. "I am so very sorry," he said to me. He then gazed into my mother's soft brown eyes. "You will hate me after this, but I cannot suffer the guilt a moment longer."

I snuggled against my mother's softness, content within her embrace and oblivious to the crisis unfolding as my father began his tale.

Siren. Water nymph. Sprite. Nix. Whichever name one wished to use, the outcome was always the same. The creature demanded payment of a perceived wrong. When my father told her the cost of his freedom, my mother gasped and held me tighter.

The last word of the tale fell from his lips, and he cringed at the tears swimming in my mother's eyes. He quickly looked away. His hand cradled the back of my downy infant head. "Do you see why I said nothing? Who would believe me? I find it hard to believe myself."

Her gaze, which had grown more horrified as the story had unfolded, grew somber. "You are not a man who exaggerates. You say you do not believe it, but your eyes tell me differently. If you say it happened, I believe you."

He shook his head, searching for any doubt he

could find. "It cannot be real." He let his head drop, shame wreathing his face. His big hand fell away from my head. "Only a madman would relate such a tale."

Though petite, my mother held a strength which her feminine form hid well. She gently put me down, securing me in my swaddling and the cradle my father had made. Strong fingers clasped his hand and she motioned to the scars that punctuated his forearm. "And these. Are they not real? Do I share your delusion? If you say a nix attacked you, then it is true. If you say, in your desire to be free, you promised her our most precious possession, then it was done without thought of it being our child."

She released him and held his head in his hands, determined to not let him bemoan the past. She pulled his face to hers, her demand simple. "Do not give up."

"What can we do? If we do not give in, we will be cursed forever."

"Have you not thought it may be something else she desires?"

"What else could it be? You did not see her. Somehow she knew of our son."

Her gaze swept the house and landed on a hand mirror inlaid with mother of pearl. She pushed back the covers and went to the small table where the mirror lay. Picking it up, she held it out to my father. "What of this?"

He let out a bark of bitter laughter. "I do not value a looking glass."

"I do. And so might she." The hope in my mother's voice caught his attention, but before he could say anything, she dove ahead. "A creature as vain as a nix would see the value in her own reflection."

"My love...I do not think—"

"Let me try." She picked up a shawl and gathered it around her shoulders, her gaze bright and determined.

"The mist is rising. Stay and acquaint yourself with your son. He needs your love as much as I do." She left before he could utter a complaint.

The night air slithered against her bare feet and ankles as the moon shot silvery blades of light through the tree branches and across the water. My mother stepped to the very edge of the lake. Her gaze probed the night, looking far and near for any sign of the nix.

The mirror lay heavy in her hands, and as she glanced down at it, she caught sight of her desperate reflection. "Let this be enough."

She knelt at the edge of the gentle ebb and flow of the lake, its cool waters chilling and mysterious as it nudged at her knees. She held out her treasure, for it truly was a thing of great value, a wedding present and dear to her. Few women could claim such a prize.

The mist hovered near. My mother searched the waves for the shape of a woman. Minutes passed, and the mist grew thicker, drew closer. My mother thought she heard a splash. The water lapped higher, dampening her nightgown even more. Was it the nix? Her heart thudded as she placed the mirror at the water's edge and looked out toward the undulating mist. "You cannot have him. Take this with my blessing and be gone."

Minutes passed. The mist swirled and grew heavy. It collected on her clothing, wetting her hair and coating her skin. With each breath, she felt smothered. She had walked the mist before, but never had she felt so threatened.

Frightened, she rose and returned to the cottage.

The next morning, as she sat brushing her hair into a gleaming veil, my father brought the shattered mirror inside. My mother stared at it and worried her bottom lip. The mirror looked as if it had been dashed against the rocks.

My father carefully placed it on the bed. "Maybe an animal stepped on it." But it was clear he didn't believe his own words.

She continued to brush her hair and stare out the window toward the lake, refusing to look at the treasure she had lost to an angry hand. They were too poor to move and too proud to beg. The nix was their burden to bear and theirs alone. "Do not lose hope. I will find something to tempt her, and she will be gone."

My father's gaze landed on me, a chubby, perfect newborn. The truth rested uneasily in his eyes. He was afraid. Without a word, he left. That afternoon, he took an ax to the boat and burned the remnants down to ash.

Thus, I was born into a world where reality and myth lived side-by-side. From the moment of my birth, the story of the nix was whispered into my ear—a warning of harm, a plea for understanding. If only the tale had stayed close, but my parents' fear had given it wings, and a slightly *altered* tale had spread throughout the village telling of the nix who had taken one look at the stonemason's newborn son and had desired him for her own. The lake grew cold and lonely as people whispered of a curse. No one even dared mention the nix for fear her anger would find them as well.

At first I obeyed the command to never go near the lake, just as I accepted my mother's offerings always ended up broken and abused the next morning. With her strange rituals and the knowledge that many had drowned in the lake, it was enough to sufficiently scare a small child into obedience.

But year after year, as I grew from toddler to young lad, the music of the lake seduced me closer. The water lapped at the shore, innocent and empty of evil...and I began to doubt.

3

The Lad That Wasn't

By necessity, the woods stretching out from my home to the boundaries of the village had become my playground. I delved into the quiet shelter and managed more mischief than a lad had a right to find. I was fearless. Climbing, digging and generally causing havoc with my surroundings. The village lads and I were great explorers. There was Gordie and Tait—the eldest of our troupe—followed by Cyril and Douglas, and then myself. The five of us found fox holes and rabbit lairs. We set traps and built hideouts and chased the girls away. All save one. Gordie's little sister. Since Gordie no longer had a mother, it fell to him to look after her while his father worked. He taught her to pee standing up—not such a good idea, but how were we to know?—and to belch and spit, at which she excelled. We cut off her hair and dressed her in hand-me-downs and called her "lad", forgetting her true name altogether.

A blood pact was called for. Even then we didn't leave her out, though Tait suggested we should. I would have none of that.

"It's all of us or none of us," I said.

The other's nodded and he caved, but with a warning. He got right into the lad's face and whispered darkly, "There's no turning back once this is done. You talk about this and you'll die."

The lad's large eyes widened and she nodded. "I'll not breathe a word."

Satisfied, Tait pulled out a long knife. It glinted evilly as it caught a stray shaft of light. I exchange a quick, nervous glance with the lad, but neither of us pulled away as the sharp blade slid across our right palms leaving a bright red streak in its wake. The lad did wince when the blade skittered across her skin, but she didn't cry, and we all gave her a hearty back slap.

With our hands dripping blood, we surrounded an old oak tree and laid our palms flat against the bark. "Now say after me," Tait murmured gravely. "Upon my own death …"

"Upon my own death …"

"I swear by holy God …"

"Should we really swear by God?" I rushed to say.

"Yes," they all shouted at me.

"This is a serious pact," Tait reminded me. "We have to. It's the law."

Being twelve, he seemed to know far more than I did. "Fine," I relented. "I was just wondering …"

"Say it," Tait demanded. "I swear by holy God…"

We repeated his words.

"Never, ever will I ever marry a girl, or even look at one kindly…"

"Never, ever will I ever marry a girl, or even look at one kindly…"

"And if I do…"

"And if I do…"

"May I be eviscerated and my insides be fed to the dogs."

"May I be eviscerated…"

"What's eviscerated?" the lad asked.

"Shut up," we all cried, and continued with the pact, "… and my insides be fed to the dogs."

"Amen," Tait concluded and pulled his hand from the tree.

With somber faces, we echoed the last word. I grabbed my hand and shook it. The bark had dug into the cut and it now burned something awful.

Before I could wipe it clean, the lad held out her hand to me. "You and me, forever," she whispered in somber imitation of Tait's voice.

We were a team. Apart we were just regular kids, but together we were unbeatable, unstoppable. I nodded, clamping her hand in mine and feeling the blood slick against our palms. "'Til death."

A huge grin transformed the lad's face. She turned to the group who were milling around unmindful of us as usual. "We got sweet cakes at the house," she piped up cheerily. "Who wants some?"

We all perked up at that, and I immediately forgot about my slick, stinging palm. I challenged the lad to a race back to the village. She won, but I didn't mind. Though scrawny, she was a scrapper and a right fine lad, and my best mate. I held no secret from her and she none from me.

For the next several years, our group was an unkempt lot—dirty and ragged and gloriously happy.

But then, Gordie's father remarried. The event caught us all off guard. Why, after all these years, would he do something so stupid as to find a new wife? The answer was clear that first night. He believed his children needed a mother. What a strange idea. We feared for our friends, so the rest of us lads snuck up on the cottage and peered into the windows.

"What happened to her, Husband?" the woman asked, inspecting the girl in lad's clothing. "I thought when first we met, you had two sons. The filth...why it's shameful. No more cutting her hair and dressing her in trews."

Their father only shrugged and said, "She is your problem now. Do what you can, but I doubt it will be much. She's grown wild running with the village lads since she was five. Your efforts'll be like pruning a hundred year old oak. No good will come of it."

But his new wife would hear none of that. With a determined glint in her eye, she grabbed the youngest lad in our band of merry men and pulled her toward the wash basin. "When a body could grow mushrooms on the dirt covering her skin, it's well and good past time for a cleaning."

When the new wife put soap to cloth, Gordie's sister yelled and fought and made such a bother that the woman grew quite afraid. "God have mercy. It's a devil in human form," she gasped.

With a sharp kick to the new wife's shin, the lad escaped to the loft where she refused to come down. Her heroics made us all proud. But how much longer could the two of them avoid the new wife's grasp? It was hard to say.

As the rest of us crept away, Tait grunted his concern. "Mark my words, that woman has persistence written all over her."

"The lad will be fine," I touted confidently. "You'll see. Both of them will be out and about come morning."

For once I was right. The next day, harboring a nasty leg bruise and a few scratches, the new wife immediately sent the pair out as soon as the sun rose. "Good riddance to bad seeds," I heard her mutter. "And may the wolves find the pair of you."

We didn't question her change of heart. Our little world was safe. Gordie and his sister were as they had always been.

I saw the little nipper glance back and stick out her tongue. I ruffled her hair, feeling the grit against my palm as I did. "What's the matter, lad?"

"Nothing. I just wonder…what does my father see in her?"

Tait laughed. At fourteen to her eleven, he had all the answers. "Some girls aren't so bad."

"What?" both she and I yelped. Surely Tait hadn't said the unthinkable.

"They're ugly and stupid," I reminded him.

"And giggly," she added.

"They have soft skin and pretty smiles," Tait rallied.

"And long, silky hair," Gordie said with a sigh, "…and they do smell nice."

Cyril and Douglas nodded while the lad and I shook our heads in disgust. "They're completely daft," she whispered to me.

"Completely," I agreed.

"Come on," she challenged, the long ago pact completely forgotten amid the search for fun and adventure. "I'll race you to the hideout."

Leaves crackled beneath the thundering of our feet, and the air grew cooler under the shade of the forest. Our pack divided, each on a mission given to us by Gordie and Tait. As the lad and I were setting a trap to catch a rabbit, she lifted her dirty face to mine and frowned. "Do you ever get scared?"

"Of what?"

"You know. *Her*." The word was whispered with all the solemnity of a church vow.

My hands stilled, and I looked around to see if anyone else were close.

Her hand slipped to my arm. "Don't worry. No one's here."

I shifted away from the lad, irritated by the question. Why did she want to know? She was always funny like that. Wanting to know what I felt. How I saw things as if the world through my eyes was any different than the one through hers. I covered a long section of string with dirt and leaves aware she hadn't stopped staring. She wouldn't until I answered her.

"No." I muttered.

She sighed. "You are very brave. I think I would be." She then grabbed a sliver of string and attached a limp piece of lettuce to it before tying the string to a stick.

I swallowed, my mind clicking on an idea that had stewed in my brain for a long time. "Don't tell anyone, but –"

Her attention was immediate. "I won't. You know you can trust me."

"I don't think it's true."

"What?" Shock played upon her face. "Your parent's lied?"

It was the one thing I couldn't understand. My parents never lied. They were good and honest…

I vehemently shook my head. "I don't think so, but it doesn't seem real. Have you ever seen the nix? Has anyone?"

"Tiller has." Tait said as he pushed through the brush. I popped to my feet, and the lad threw me a look

28

of apology as the rest of the boys filed in behind him.

Cyril glanced around nervously. "You shouldn't talk about that."

Gordie shook his head. "You're an idiot, Tait. Everyone knows old man Tiller's crazy. I bet if I told him I seen a fox do a jig, he'd say he'd seen one, too."

"My father says Ryne's father is a nutter." Everyone turned to stare at Douglas. The boy's gaze bounced around the group. "Well he did."

I could feel my ears burn with anger, but before I could act, the lad jumped forward and pushed Douglas. "You're father is the nutter." A light scuffle between the two ensued before Gordie and I broke it up.

The lad struggled to be free in my hands. "Let me go," she growled.

"It doesn't matter," I whispered in her ear.

The lad whipped her face toward mine, her lips a tight line. "It should."

Her dark look told me it was too late. Her temper had ignited. She jerked free, and her attention quickly flew to where Tait inspected the construction of our trap. "Don't you dare touch anything, you toad."

Tait tossed back an unconcerned look. "Nice trap." He ran his finger along the stick that held the lure. His eyes suddenly brightened. "That's it. We could build a boat and see for ourselves if the tale is true."

The lad stepped forward, right in the middle of the trap, stomping it apart amid the boys yells to get off. "Are you mad?" she screamed into Tait's face. "We'll not use Ryne as bait."

Tait's gaze whipped to Gordie's. "I hadn't thought of that. You know, I think it could work. How fast can we build a boat?"

The lad head-butted Tait, and the two fell to the

ground. The boys burst out laughing at the sight of the tiny lad whooping on the bigger boy. My jaw tightened, and I shot an accusing glance at the group. I shouldn't care what they said, but the teasing had grown, and it was beginning to wear on me. As the fight continued, I slipped away and headed home.

My mother glanced up from her sewing, a questioning look on her face, when I burst through the front door. I put my head down and ran for my room where I threw myself onto the bed and glared out the window. A moment later, I saw the lad break free of the tree line and saw Gordie follow. He caught up with her and pulled her away.

Good thing. I didn't want to talk. I didn't want to hear another word about the nix.

The creak of the door sounded and the bed sagged as my mother sat next to me. Her cool fingers slipped through my hair. "What's wrong?"

"Nothing."

She sighed. "The weight of your nothing is very definitely something."

I flipped onto my back and propped myself up on my elbows. "Did father lie?"

"I don't understand—"

"About the nix. Did he lie?"

She worried at her bottom lip for a brief second. "Your father never lies."

"Then you really believe I'll die?"

"No." Horror at what I said blossomed on her face. "I will not let you die. So long as you stay away from the—"

"They're laughing at me. They think we're crazy…as crazy as old man Tiller."

Her hand stilled, and she pulled it away. "I'm

sorry."

Her voice had grown muted, sad and ineffective at chasing away the hurt.

I rolled back onto my stomach and glared out the window, tucking my pillow beneath my chin. "I just want it to stop."

"I know." She put her hand on my back and I flinched, willing her away. A moment later, she left. Nothing would ever change. My parents still believed. The curse still lingered. And in everyone's eyes, I was still doomed.

"You're an idiot."

The tiny voice came from outside my window. I got up and dangled my torso over the sill, and there sat the lad—an excellent escape artist—leaning against my house, her dirty hands resting on her boney knees.

"What do you mean?"

She didn't look up, but stared out toward the forest. "Why don't you fight back?"

"I don't know."

"I'll tell you why. You believe the curse."

My heart suddenly began to hammer in my chest. "I do not."

She cocked her head and glanced up at me. "Then show them you don't."

"How?"

A mischievous smile rippled against her mouth. "We'll find a way." The lad jumped to her feet and faced me. "Come on. Gordie dared Tait to swim out into the lake. For all his talk, he nearly pissed himself. I say he don't got the guts." Her fingers gripped the stone sill and she leaned forward, her face suddenly serious. "Truth, Ryne. None of them do."

"Really?" I climbed out of the widow and dropped

to the ground. We stared at each other for a moment, and then I offered a truce. "We need to fix that snare."

The lad nodded. "Did you see me hit Tait? I think I cracked his big ugly nose." I congratulated her on the accomplishment as we took off toward the forest.

Oh, the carefree years of youth. They swept me along until one day, I was fourteen, the lad thirteen, and we were sitting in a tree waiting for someone to come down the path so we could spit on their heads. It was one of the less obnoxious games we played. All our mates had grown up and were forced to work for their fathers until they could be apprenticed to tradesmen in other villages. Just the lad and I were left to amuse ourselves. I turned to her and leaned close for a whisper. "There's someone com—"

The words froze on my lips.

Somehow, a ray of sunlight had found its way into our hiding spot and managed to pour all its warmth on the lad. It was as if she were receiving a heavenly blessing. Her hair, a common brown just moments ago, shown the color of wet tree bark and smelled of sunshine and lavender. I pulled back as if I'd been stung.

"What did you do?" I accused in no uncertain terms.

"Shhh," she scolded, "someone's coming."

Her face glowed peaches and cream and her golden flecked cheeks had grown flushed with anticipation.

"Your face. Your hair," I insisted, confused at this sudden change in her. "You smell."

She gathered a large section of hair in her hand—the strands gleamed softly in the light—and held it beneath her delicate nose. "You're daft. I don't smell anything."

"I tell you, you smell."

Heavy, uneven footsteps sounded. The interloper,

old man Tiller, glanced up at us, and quickly moved down the path at an awkward trot that had his bum leg scraping the dust into a roiling cloud. Being lame, he had been lucky enough to have been a prior victim of our youthful escapades, but as I gaped witlessly at Gordie's sister, he took his chance to get away unscathed. I didn't care. I was solely focused on the stranger beside me.

From her, a familiar swirl of anger lashed out. "Now you've gone and chased our first victim away." She turned an accusing eye on me. "What is wrong with you?"

Sitting there, staring into her cobalt eyes, it was then I noticed how large and heavily lashed they were, and how they tilted up at the outer corners mysteriously.

My gaping mouth must have amused her for her anger vanished as quickly as it had come, and she threw me a mischievous grin, nudging me in the arm. "You did that apurpose, didn't you? You've grown soft. You know, he expects it to happen. Now what will he have to talk about over his ale but his crazy tales of nymphs and gnomes and tiny faeries?"

I heard nary a word of what she said. My gaze had dropped to her moving lips–rosy and lush and kissable sweet.

I suddenly couldn't breathe. Images of our lips touching invaded my mind. I dug my fingertips into the rough bark beneath me and launched off the limb, scrambling down the tree as fast as I could. Only when I reached the ground did I feel safe enough to look up.

My friend had gone.

In a flash of a moment, the lad had disappeared to be replaced by a…a…*girl*. The prettiest girl I'd ever seen.

The mysterious creature cocked her head and openly stared back. "What is wrong with you, Ryne? Have I grown long ears and buck teeth?"

Worse. She had grown up. But how could that be? I was still a lad, and a full year older than her. It couldn't be.

The light was bad. That was all. Were those not the same clothes she wore yesterday?

"Come down here, Nari."

She blinked, a look of shock on her face. "What did you say?"

"Come down."

She scampered down the tree trunk nearly as quickly and skillfully as I. When her feet touched the ground, she turned to me. Nope. The lad was gone. I backed up, unsure of the creature before me.

"You called me Nari."

The condemnation in her gaze caught me off guard and I bristled back, "It's your name, isn't it?"

"You never call me that."

"You took a bath."

She crinkled up her nose and pushed her long hair out of her face. "I've taken one ever since I was eleven."

The muted light coming through the trees highlighted her as if she were a precious jewel. When had her hair grown so long and beautiful? "You smell, I say, and I don't like it."

It was a lie. I liked it all too well, and it terrified me.

Confusion crossed her features. With a great deal of irritation, she planted her fists on her hips. Like a hound on the scent of fresh blood, she narrowed her eyes. "How so?"

"Like flowers. Like a *girl*."

I might as well have slapped her in the face. She grew deathly pale and her kissable lips quivered ever so slightly. I couldn't have shocked her more.

I wanted to protect her. I wanted to hold her. I

wanted to never let her go. And in wanting her, I felt the blood seep from my own face as I grew lightheaded. I felt sick in the pit of my belly. What was happening to me? I pointed a shaky finger at her. "You stay away from me, you hear? Just stay away."

I couldn't look at her anymore. In the face of my fear, I turned and ran.

4

Alone But Not Forgotten

My feet took me toward home. Always a refuge, but now, once I saw the small cottage, I knew I could not go inside. There would be questions. Too many, and most I did not want to answer. Instead, I turned deeper into the woods that skirted my home. The tang of pine, the mustiness of wet earth and rotting leaves and the sweet spice of honeysuckle greeted me. After an hour of pushing through the dense foliage, I wandered closer to the lake and stumbled onto an amazing sight.

I stood rooted to the spot as the alarm, which had been instilled in me since I was born, reared forward. A watery oasis—deep, indigo pool, high, frothing waterfall—unfolded before me, yet I could not move for fear my feet would take me straight to the water, and to my death.

How could I not have known of this place? I allowed my gaze to roam the site, noting how the trees hugged the shore, curtaining the waterfall from anyone passing by on the lake. With the thick foliage surrounding it, I could see how it had remained untouched. If my friends had known about this place, they would have forced me here long ago in hopes they could break me of my fear.

I let out a shaky breath, releasing the tension I held tightly inside. I'd always been drawn to water, but at that moment, a sudden enchantment fell over me and I fell in love. Voicing its own language, the rumble of water lured me closer, calling me.

The appearance of falling water was an anomaly I couldn't figure out. There was no river nearby, and to suddenly see water pouring from the earth in such violent, rushing splendor perplexed me. It took me no time at all to climb the slate cliffs. On closer inspection, it appeared as if a deep spring forced the water to the surface and over the edge of the escarpment. Legend had it that our lake, and its siblings close by, were made by an ancient creature so massive, that when it ran, its footprint formed yawning pits as it pushed the landscape into tall cliffs and yawning pits. The earth, under such violent force, opened the wells of the deep and water sprang forth, filling the pits.

If one believed Tait—and one would have to be a complete dolt to believe everything *he* said—a man could dive deep under the water and find jewel encrusted caves that stretched halfway around the world.

After our group had heard this latest twist to the old legend—for Tait loved to tell tall tales, especially when we waited for our next victim to walk by—Gordie shook his head. "That's the biggest lie you've said yet."

"It's the truth," Tait swore from his side of the trap we'd set. "They say that's why Ryne's father was out on the lake. Stealing the nix's treasure. Everyone knows they are as poor as poor can be."

The group grew still at the mention of the nix. For all their talk, they feared the curse. Leave it to Douglas to dare a curse. Hidden in the brush next to Tait and Cyril, he glanced over at me from across the lane. "So why does she want ol' Ryne, then?"

"He's right helpful, that's why." The lad clamped me on the shoulder as she spoke out in my defense. She turned to me, her dirt smudged face showing its worry. "Maybe she wants you to polish her jewels?"

I didn't like it when the topic turned to my family. Our lack of fortune was hardly news. And talk of the nix only embarrassed me. Stuck fast between Gordie and his little sister, I could only shrug and pray I could convince them to drop the subject. "Wealth is measured by experience, not coin," I said, repeating my father's litany. "And there is no nix. It's just a silly story, one to keep me safe from drowning." And one, that over the years, I'd learned to hate.

"Then you won't mind going for a swim after this, eh Ryne?"

I glared over at Tait. "Only if you go, too." I didn't wait to hear his reply. "I've got to go." I pushed off the ground amid the lad's hisses to leave me be and headed back home, my heart triple beating with just the thought of wading in the lake.

Yet now, as I stood atop the escarpment and looked through the break in the trees to the lake, I noticed how its surface sparkled crystal blue and green and deep purple. I could almost imagine a cave with shimmering jewels that colored the water so prettily. Why had I ever been scared?

I dropped my gaze to this hidden place, a pool attached to the lake, yet hidden and all my own. Scattered among the massive trees with limbs so large that many drooped to the ground from sheer weight, lay huge ferns, their width big enough to cradle a grown man and soft-spined brush sprinkled with purple and blue flowers. Springy moss seemed to cover nearly every rock and tree, cushioning my steps as I explored.

I quickly climbed down, feeling more at home than I had anywhere else, and threw myself onto the moss covered ground—not too close to the pool—and listened to the music of the waterfall. As I sank into the rhythm of the forest, the creatures I'd chased away with my unexpected arrival crawled back, accepting this lump of being that only lay quietly by the pooling water. If the lad could see me now, she would beg me to leave, insisting it was unwise to tempt fate.

I frowned. There was no lad. The mischievous tag-a-long I knew as my best friend was no more. Deep down, I knew the lad was gone for good.

How had it happened? What was I to do?

The water pounded the last question into my head, but offered no easy solution. I gently kneaded the soft moss with my fingertips as I eased my left arm under my head and stared through the thick canopy of leaves. I frowned, thinking of what had happened and realizing with a fair degree of alarm that I was alone, the last merry man of our forest.

Anger welled up within me. How dare she turn into a girl.

Nari was a girl.

A real girl.

A pretty girl.

A *very* pretty girl.

Unsettled by the trail of my thoughts, I flopped onto my side, scaring the creatures into hiding again. I gave little thought to those I disturbed, and gazed at the water bouncing off the stones until the churning mass tumbled into the pool. *What to do?...What to do?...What to do?* the gurgle and plunge repeated over and over again.

I listened to the question for a long time, until my limbs grew heavy and my eyes slowly closed against the creeping mist rolling in. Sleep greeted me with a painful truth.

The lad had always been a girl. I'd created an illusion to suit my needs, just as my parents had created a nix to keep me from the water. In my dream Nari turned into a beautiful water nymph, and we swam around the lake until I grew tired and began to drown. As I pleaded for her help, she only smiled and circled me and laughed as water filled my lungs.

I awoke, gasping for air. Though my eyes were open, my vision was foggy and unfocused, and for a moment, I thought I had seen...had seen...someone. I blinked and rubbed at my eyes, but the fogginess was a mist that had settled into the cove. I eased myself to a sitting position and gazed out over the mist shrouded pool, searching for what had caught my eye. The water near the falls churned and bubbled, but the rest of the pool lay still and quiet. It had probably been a shadow cast by a passing bird.

As I glanced around the area, I noticed a decided dip in the moss near the water's edge. On closer inspection, it had all the hallmarks of an imprint which ended just a few inches from where I lay. I frowned and bent closer, checking the ground nearest me where the moss had been scratched away to reveal the dull brown earth. I traced my finger along the ridges, ridges that looked like long, scratches

They reached just shy of my resting place.

A fine joke. Had my friends followed me here? Was there no place I could find peace? I jerked my head up. "Tait? Douglas? Cyril?" Those friends would find it a great laugh to scare me like this. They all knew the story of the nix and had teased me to no end. "Gordie?" Had he already heard how I embarrassed myself with Nari? Was this his great plan to get even with me for upsetting his sister?

Again I cried out their names, but no hushed laughs echoed back, only the muffled rush and plummet of the water and the beasts of the forest. I placed my hand on the springy green clumps. The moss felt cool...and soaking wet. My gaze returned to the water.

A recollection dashed across my minds' eye. A vision upon my waking just moment's past. I concentrated, pulling the foggy memory into focus. A person. Sort of. More like a vague outline of someone obscured by the patchy mist, hovering for just a second in the water. My heart leapt to my throat. Someone...or something had tried to reach me while I slept. A shiver spiraled down my spine, and the last trace of grogginess disappeared. I jumped up. With widened eyes, I looked down. Just like with a feather mattress, a perfect outline of a body had been pressed into the moss.

It wasn't a nix. It couldn't be. The tale was a figment of my father's delirious mind. Still, the enchantment of the area faded, and I eased away from my resting place and into the forest where the soft touch of green and the scratch of bark held more familiar sensations than that of sparkling water and unexplainable wet moss.

It took me a while to find my way home in the fading light, but when I got there, I found Gordie and Tait waiting.

"Oi," Gordie cried out, his face alive with emotion as he gave me a thump to my chest. "What did you do to my sister?"

It was late and I was in a foul mood. I felt my jaw tighten, still carrying the remnants of alarm I experienced when I lay at the water's edge. "You trying to scare me, Gordie? That was a great laugh back there, but you'll have to do more than that to put me off."

"Why you thick-headed little mongrel," he growled, slapping me on the back of my head. "Don't you go putting *me* off. I asked you a bloody question. What did you do?"

I got right into his face, my nose to his chin, and snarled back, "I will not be bullied."

Tait stepped between us. "Easy, lads. You know a girl can get all excited about nothing. Now, Gordie, let poor Ryne say what he needs to say." He turned to me and nodded encouragingly. "Go on. What happened?"

Tait was a tricky one. When I thought he was on my side, he'd often turn at the last minute and bring me low. He was the exact opposite of Gordie's dark, brooding good looks, yet no less handsome. The pair made all the girls swoon when they walked by. It was disgusting.

"I didn't do anything to her," I snapped.

"Then why's she crying?" Gordie demanded to know.

Nari was crying? My stomach tightened, but I refused to let it bother me. I shrugged as if I cared naught for her tears. "How would I know?"

"I saw you running toward your house…and then there she comes, not more than a moment later, all teary." He shoved a finger into my face. "That's not a coincidence, my lad. That's proof you did something."

"We argued, all right? That's all. It's not like we've never argued before." That was true. I and the lad had argued fiercely over the years. But now? Things were different.

"You've never made her cry before."

What could I say? That I didn't know I'd left her in tears? I didn't, but what would that do? I could hardly say I found Nari to be the most beautiful girl I'd ever seen. They'd laugh.

When I finally looked up, they were staring at me. I looked from Gordie to Tait, and the latter's face suddenly brightened. "You tried to kiss her, didn't you?"

Shock rocked me back on my heels. I hadn't but I'd wanted to. "I did not," I choked out sounding as horrified as I felt.

"Why not?" Gordie, asked, sounding offended that I hadn't.

They couldn't know the chaos Nari had thrown me into. My life would be misery if they did. I scrambled for a defense. Screwing up my face, I sprang forward, slamming into Tait's chest as I yelled over his shoulder toward Gordie, "I would as much kiss her as I would you, you ugly puss."

"Oh-ho…" Tait said with a knowing look as he grabbed my arm and pushed me back. "I understand now. Our little man likes her."

Gordie's face suddenly lost all its anger. "What? Is that what this is? You like Nari?"

"I don't," I insisted. They had to believe me. If they didn't, I'd…I'd…die.

Tait's smile grew even wider. "Look at him, all red-faced and bug-eyed. He likes her all right, and it scared her to tears."

I slammed my fist into the bigger lad's upper arm.

"Shut up, Tait."

My hit didn't faze him one bit. He only cast a glance back at Gordie. "Yep, sounds like a lad who wanted a kiss, but didn't have the stomach to take it. Sad, that. I thought we taught him better."

"Watch it, Tait," Gordie said with a frown. "That's my sister you're talking about."

I felt sick inside. Suddenly, all I wanted was to lie down and cry myself to sleep. What kind of a rough and tumble lad would admit to that? Instead, I broke free of Tait's restraining hand and turned away. "Go off with you. I don't want to talk anymore."

Tait yanked me into a head lock and raked his knuckles across my head. "Aww, come on. Give us a smile. It's not the first time you will be greeted with disgust when you go for a kiss and a cuddle."

"Let him be, Tait," Gordie said, pulling his best friend off me. "Why don't you go on? I'll be right behind you."

"You sure?" Tait pushed his blond hair out of his eyes. "I would hate to hear tomorrow how you beat poor Ryne into an early grave."

"On my word," Gordie swore, "I'll not hurt him."

"Right, then." Tait cuffed me on the side of my head. "If he feints left, well…I guess that means he lied and you'll be dead by morning. Good luck with that." And he strode away.

Some friend he was. I didn't trust Gordie, so why did he?

I backed up. My house was only a few yards away. My legs were shorter than Gordie's, but I'd always been faster than him. I could be inside behind a locked door before he even took his first step. "I mean it, Gordie. I won't talk about it. You might as well leave."

He shook his head and rolled his eyes. "Stop moving around like that. I gave my word no harm would come to you."

I gave measure to his words and the sincerity in which he spoke them, and I finally managed to stand still.

"That's better," he said, and then, "There's nothing wrong with you liking my sister."

I cautiously watched him take a step forward, and I prepared to run. He noticed and stopped. "You're as skittish as a fox caught in the hen house, but you needn't be."

"I'm fine. I swear I'll never like her."

"You swear? Is that it then? Do you fear the pact?" He laughed. "That was a stupid thing we did. But rest assured, you won't die tomorrow. God knows boys are stupid. He won't hold you to it."

"I know that." But I still felt a deep sickness in my belly that I couldn't explain. All I knew was that my best friend was gone and had never really existed.

Gordie cocked his head thoughtfully. "Good. Because of all the lads I know, I'd rather you like Nari than them."

"You're talking to air," I blurted out. I didn't like this Gordie, the lad who talked gently and could see right through me. Was my sudden love for Nari that obvious? "I told you, I don't like her, and I most definitely did *not* try and kiss her."

"Fine. If that's the way you want it." He turned to leave, but then turned back. "I'll be expecting you to apologize. You hurt her feelings, you know."

As he turned and walked away, I felt the world grow heavy upon my shoulders. "I know." But I couldn't apologize. Not yet.

5

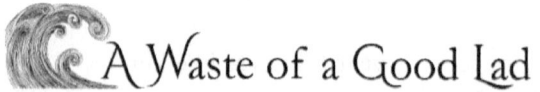

A Waste of a Good Lad

I would like to say I quickly forgave Nari of the change. But I didn't. It was a betrayal of the worst kind. She had been a lad for so long, and a right fine lad to boot, that to see her any other way was a shock. But there she was, day after day, a girl. No one but me seemed to see Nari in her new form. She came and went with as much notice as she had always generated—none at all.

But not to me. I knew the moment she was near. I felt her presence like a living touch that had me cowering in the oddest places.

A few weeks after I'd given her up for good, Nari waylaid me in the market, behind the tanner's hut. "Why won't you talk to me?" She snarled in my face.

I should have known the rancid stench of wet animal skins and rotting flesh wouldn't have put her off like other girls. She grabbed my arm, her strong fingers digging into my muscle as she voiced her desperate plea. "What did I do wrong?"

I shook off her hand. "Nothing."

She moved into my line of vision, and my gaze darted past her, focusing on the street vendor selling plump meat pasties.

It was true. *Nari* had done nothing purposely. My mother had explained to me how life never stayed the same. Even I would change and there was little I could do about it. All the other lads had gone, and Nari and I had made a pact to never leave each other. A wishful illusion. When I looked at Nari, I was forced to see my future, and the thought of growing up scared me, for the only future I possessed was one pointing toward death.

"Then why won't you talk to me? Even now you won't look at me. Am I really so ugly?"

My heart pounded within my chest. Had Gordie or Tait told her what I'd said that day outside my house? I spoke out of defense. How could she not know how breathtaking she looked with the sun painting gold on her hair and the light of mischief in her eyes? I swallowed down the silly words of praise and forced out a bitter lie. "I have nothing to say to you...ever."

Desperation filled the tight alley. "Ryne, you are my best friend. I cannot lose you."

"I am *not* your best friend. Why don't you find some girl to talk to?"

"What? You know how I feel about them. They're silly, stupid creatures."

"They are just like you."

She stiffened and said in a choked voice, "Take that back."

She wanted too much from me. Unlike her, I was still just a lad. I couldn't allow the strange feelings she conjured to return. Concentrating on the dips and grooves on the uneven ground, I told her what my heart did not wish to say. "I cannot be your friend, Nari. Please try and understand. I cannot."

After a moment of strained silence, a strangled hiccough sounded, and I made the mistake of looking up at her. Big, luminous eyes filled with tears until one escaped and rolled fat and wet down her perfect cheek.

Horrified, I watched another race after the first. "Stop it," I whispered huskily. "Stop it."

"I can't," she moaned.

My belly grew hot, and the feeling rushed to my face and tightened my lips. I would be sick. "Leave me alone. Just...leave me alone."

I roughly pushed her against the wall and darted out into the bustle of the market. Needed items were forgotten in my rush to find a safe haven where I could will my heart to slow and my face to cool.

Nari was not one to give up so easily. She could be like a terrier after a rat, sniffing and digging until she cornered her quarry and nipped at it until she got what she wanted. And Nari typically got what she wanted. So I vowed to disappear, to lay low and quiet and wait for her to give up the chase.

And she did, though not by her own want. With her husband's hard-won consent, the new wife sent Nari off to a cousin's to refine her wifery skills. It was a last ditch effort to "civilize her," the new wife had been heard saying. "God knows I have done what I could," she complained to a pocketful of her cronies. "But bad seed being what it is, there is little hope she'll come back with any real talent or hope of a husband."

From my hiding place, I glared at the new wife. I wanted to tell that hateful woman right then and there that Nari had more talent than any female I knew. She could swing a fist more accurately, snare a rabbit easier, and run faster than all us lads combined. But it would do no good. The new wife was determined to see her 'strange' step-daughter go. From my hiding place, I watched Nari search the crowd, and saw her shoulders droop when they loaded her and her things into an old cart that carried her off to a village half a week's ride away.

I should have been happy to see her off, but misery closed in on me and wouldn't let me go. I thought I should go mad thinking of her. What was she doing? Who was she with? Did she think of me? Did she even care?

I hated this new weakness that had me lying awake at night listening to the heavy breathing of my parent's fill the house. Even the lap of water against the lake's shore couldn't soothe me. What was wrong with me that I would turn away from my best friend? I felt deceived. I had bit on the illusion she had built, yet I'd conveniently forgotten my part in its creation.

Sensing my despair, my father pulled me aside one day. "I heard tell the smithy is in need of a lad."

"A good job, Ryne," my mother piped in. And far from the lake, her gaze relayed.

"He's a good man, that Jack," my father announced. "Go. An apprenticeship is just what you need."

The opportunity held little inspiration. "I would rather work with you." And far away from the gossip.

"And I would rather you make money than ease my work. Off with you, now."

Though I'd rather not go, I went. The ping and grunt of the smithy met me before I entered the shop. The usual crowd gathered close, men darkened by the sun, and honed by a long, hard days' work. My father was right. There was money to be made with the constant flow of plows to fix, wheels to mend and horses to shoe. The men saw me coming and parted, each hesitating to get too close. I pretended not to notice how they fell silent and how their stares followed me. I lingered on the edge, awaiting my chance to speak to Jack.

The smithy pounded out a smooth rhythm. Muscles rolled and sweat glistened as the big man labored to mold the iron clamped between the iron tongs. I was still but a runt of a boy. What could possibly be expected of me in a place like this?

Jack stopped, and wiped his brow, and looked up when he noticed the heavy silence. When he saw me, a look of alarm passed before he shuttered his emotions. "Ryne. What brings you here?"

An endeavor more hopeless could not be found, but I stepped forward and nodded my greeting. "My father heard you are offering an apprenticeship."

An indistinct noise rose from the men, and Jack cast a quick glance their way. "I-I am…"

"Inviting disaster, Jack, that's what you are if you take on this lad," Cyril's father said.

"Aye," came the rumble of agreement.

"Who would trust him?" a deep voice near the back of the crowd asked.

"I would work hard," I offered, trying my best to ignore their claim.

"Until the day he disappears," someone shouted.

"Inviting the curse in your home, Jack," Cyril's father warned.

The smithy's face paled. He turned unyielding eyes on me as his gripped tightened against the heavy hammer he held. "I need no curse from a dead lad on my hands. Go on with you. Tell your father to foist you off on someone else."

My body had grown tense. An unexpected pang swelled within my chest. He spoke as if I were already dead. As if I were an unwelcome spirit bent on evil.

Distrusting glares pierced my skin. Angry whispers assaulted my ears. I slowly backed away, and then turned and ran.

My father looked up from the stone he was splitting when I approached. His cheerful greeting faded with one look at me. "What did he say?" Though he knew it was not good.

I kept walking. He shot a hand out and pulled me to a halt. We stared at each other for a long time. My breathing had yet to settle from fear and the run home.

"Well?" he prodded.

"He doesn't want a dead lad working for him."

His fingers tightened on my arm. "What are you talking about?"

"Me," I shouted. "They fear the curse. Don't you get it? Your stupid tale has ruined my life."

He pulled away, confusion highlighting his weathered features. "No. They misunderstand. You misunderstand. I'll talk to them. I'll make sure they—"

"They won't listen. They're afraid. You have made them all afraid." I took a step forward and then stopped. "Never speak of her to me again."

He needn't ask of whom I spoke. From that moment on, the tale of the nix would no longer find a place in my life. I began helping my father with his stone work the next day. I eased his physical burden, but not our woes, for money still eluded us no matter how hard we toiled.

Without my best friend by my side, the looks and whispers of the villagers closed in on me. Visiting the village made my stomach churn. Mothers pulled their children indoors when they saw me. At first I thought nothing of it until one afternoon, my mother dragged me to the Market, a convenient pack mule for her mounting provisions. As I quietly followed her from stall to stall, I accidentally bumped into a girl admiring some ribbons with two of her friends. The three gasped.

"Pardon me," I muttered, and shot a quick glance at the girl to make sure I hadn't hurt her.

A collection of giggles rose from the group, and the one I'd knocked into peeked up at me from behind a dark span of thick eyelashes. "I'm fine, thank you."

She was pretty in that girly way girls look. The other two were repeats in dress, hair and giggles. I could feel my cheeks burn under their combined feminine stares. I nodded and hurried after my mother. As I slowed, I heard the quick clatter of feet on cobblestones hurrying behind me. I glanced back and straight at the girls. They abruptly stopped, their skirts swaying against their ankles, and their fingers twirling their hair as another round of giggles bubbled forth.

What was wrong with them? I didn't know what to do, so I threw them a hesitant smile.

The one I'd bumped into stepped forward. "You're Ryne, aren't you?"

A lump knotted my stomach. "Y-yes." I glanced to where I expected my mother to be, but she had moved on. I was torn between following her and staying under the warm stares of these girls.

"My brother used to talk about you all the time. You and the other boys, that is."

That was a good hint. I knew her brother. But it didn't help. I hadn't noticed a girl besides Nari in forever, and I was having a hard time placing these. "He did?"

She nodded and the other girls giggled and clasped

hands nervously.

"She thinks you're handsome," the petite blonde blurted out, and her attached companion playfully slapped at her.

The pretty one shot the traitor a hateful look.

The declaration caught me so off guard, I nearly dropped the packages I carried. "Oohh, I-I—"

"You made him blush," the other girl chirped. And the three burst into another fit of giggles.

"What's going on here?" Douglas approached with a frown planted firmly on his face. He took one look at my flaming face and then at his sister staring googlie-eyed at me and her friends all atwitter, and his temper mounted. "Go home, the lot of you."

"You can't boss me around," his sister said with a stamp of her foot.

"Yes I can."

"I'm telling Mother and she'll tell Fa—"

"And he'll tan my hide if he finds out I let you make an goose out of yourself drooling over the likes of him," he said, nodding his head in my direction.

His adamant stance made her cast a wary glance in my direction. "What's wrong with him?"

The blush drained from my face and the knot twisted painfully in my gut. I knew what he was going to say and there was no way I could stop him.

"He's cursed."

The petite blonde made a strange, strangling sound. "*He's* the one everyone's talking about?" She took a huge step back, tugging the other girls back with her. "Come on. Douglas is right. Let's go."

I watched as the girls fearfully scurried out of sight. When they were gone, Douglas slanted an angry look at me that made the freckles on his face glow unattractively.

He bent close and snarled, "Stay away from my sister."

With his warning ringing in my ears, he stalked away.

I glanced around and saw a handful of people staring at me, accusingly, but of what, I had no idea. I just knew it bode ill for me if I continued to stand there alone. I quickly sought out my mother and begged her to go home.

Ostracized by the adults and rejected by my peers, I found my life unbearable living in the shadow of my impending doom. I refused to go to market. I stayed away from people, preferring the silence of the forest to their ignorant ideas. True to their word, my parents did not speak of the nix, but every time the mist rolled in, my mother's gaze would grow haunted and my father would grow tense.

The winter of my fifteenth year, my mother took ill and I was forced to the village for supplies. It was late in the day, and I hoped most would be home preparing for supper. A misplaced hope if ever there was one. As soon as I stepped foot in town, startled glances followed me. If I kept my head down, going about my business, I would be done and gone in no time. Alas, it was just my luck that the widow Jens, who lived near Nari, stopped me on my way home only steps from the market corner.

She leaned heavily on her walking stick as her watery gaze questioned who she saw. "Is that you, Ryne?"

"It is." I said, though I would have preferred to dart past now that my errands were over and done.

She patted along my arm, her fingers sizing up my growth, and smiled. "My, my. But aren't you a nice fit lad for a lonely nix."

She cackled, and I could feel my body tense at her words. I darted my gaze down the street, seeing other's slow their steps to listen. Her breath wheezed in and out, shaking her body like a dried piece of leaf. "Obeying your parents, I see."

"I am." I hefted the items in my arms so that even she could see I was busy.

Her gaze wandered my face. "Such a shame you're cursed. You would have made a handsome man."

A tic found my cheek, and though I tried to hide it, the bite of annoyance found my voice. "Thank you."

I wriggled free and slipped quickly into the nearest door which thankfully was a darkened pub. I stood at the frosted window and peered outside at the crowd milling near the widow. I could just imagine the gossip. The tale resurrected yet again. Did they never grow tired of it?

A hand landed on my shoulder, and I twirled around. The smiling faces of Gordie and Tait stared back. Gordie let go and held out his hand. "Ryne, it's good to see you."

I took it and offered him a smile. It had been a long time since I'd shared one with a friend.

"It is," Tait added after taking a sip of his ale. "God's truth, I didn't know you were still alive."

I cast an irritated look at him and turned to Gordie. "I heard you left."

"I did. Our mule kicked Father and broke his ribs, so I'm helping with the crops until he recovers." He leaned close. "Between you and me, I miss it here."

I could not relate. If I were ever offered a position away, I would jump at it. Sadly, whenever a position opened, the villagers always managed to bring up the curse until even the smallest of opportunities open to my friends remained firmly closed to me.

"Come. Have a drink."

The publican cast a jaundiced eye on me, but seeing

as I was with Gordie and Tait, he said naught. We sat at a table and within the hour we were arm wrestling like we used to do when we were young. Though Gordie and Tait were eight and ten, I beat them both two out of three tries thanks to the back breaking work of hauling huge stones and splitting them all day.

Gordie laughed off his loss good naturedly, and we fell into an easy companionship. No mention of Nari passed between us. He seemed to understand the growing pains I continued to endure when it came to her.

Tait was another matter entirely. He wallowed in his loss, and his drink, until he slammed his tankard on the table. "How about a swim?" Tait lurched to his feet and yelled at the other patrons. "Would not we all like to see Ryne take a long swim in the lake?"

Gordie tugged Tait back into his seat and snarled at him to shut up, but Tait wouldn't listen. He leaned forward, his breath a nauseous mix as he challenged, "Well, Ryne? How about it?"

The smirk on his face irritated me more than the fearful stares of those listening. I downed the last of my ale and stared back. The drink sat heavy in my stomach; its false warmth colored my cheeks, but unlike Tait, my brains remained intact. "No thanks." I shot a quick glance at Gordie. "I should be getting back. It was good to see you again."

"That's right Ryne," Tait called as I headed for the door, "Run home and hide. Maybe the nix won't find you."

As his laughter filled the pub, something inside me snapped. The small ripple of irritation grew, frothy and violent. I slowly turned around. On seeing me, Tait bounded to his feet. "Have you something to say?"

I had so much whirling in my mind, I was afraid to

speak. Instead, I walked right up to Tait and placed my packages on the table. He leaned forward, his lips parted for another lie…and I slammed my fist into his jeering face. His head flew back, and like a rag doll, he folded onto the table in an unconscious heap.

I glanced around the pub, challengingly. The room grew still. No one said a word.

Gordie looked from his friend to me, the shock of what I'd done slowly registering. "Good shot, Ryne."

It felt good. I nodded my respects to the gaping publican and left.

By that summer, Tait won an apprenticeship with a miller and left for a nearby village, finally garnering me peace from his teasing, while Douglas and Cyril were kept busy working on their family farms.

I continued to help my father with the masonry, cutting stone and affixing wattle and daub. The woods still held my interest, but not in that magical, mysterious way they did when I was younger. Now when I entered them, I took bow and arrow, and a sharp skinning knife. I developed a keen eye, a good ear, and a straight shot. Little escaped my aim. So good had I become, that the butcher ignored what he called his better judgment and regularly bought my game, though he made me promise not to tell.

In my forced solitude, I found myself at the lakeside pool, more and more. The pain in my stomach had morphed into a deep loneliness, one I couldn't will away. My life had deteriorated into a tiny spot. I hadn't the smallest hope of making a living, less hope of gaining a lasting friendship and even less hope in finding true love. I had become a ghost without ever dying. Tait's challenge burned within me. I would never be accepted until I rid myself of the curse.

But how?

Sitting, I leaned against a tree and stared at the pool. The sound of falling water soothed me and I began to relax. Slowly, a vision of a world which lay beneath the water slipped into my imagination—colorful fish, strange rock formations and a system of caves, their labyrinth as intricate as any maze above ground unfolded as if I were swimming the lake waters myself.

My mind created a woman. Beautiful. Serene. Her dark locks floated freely in the current as she breathed deep the water as if it were air. With a gentle roll of her fingers, she beckoned me forward until an unnatural feeling of longing tugged at my soul.

My eyes sharpened back to reality. I sat forward, shaking my head clear, irritated by my imagination. I was tired of the fantasy my parents used to control me as a child. Raking my hair from my face, I glared at the quiet, empty pool.

"You are not real."

Then what of the vision? my innermost being demanded. It seemed so real.

The water beckoned me forward. A shudder swept my spine, yet I moved ever closer and stared harder into the pool's depths. "Convince me you are real."

Nothing happened. I slid even closer and stabbed at its surface, causing ripples to lap away from me. I grew angry at myself for ever having given in to the lie. "Come on. I am waiting. Take me if you dare."

Still nothing.

I could resist the lure of the lake no longer. Keeping my knife with me, I waded into the pool, the water lapping at my knees, my hips, and then my torso. I sank deeper and deeper, until its coolness finally swallowed my shoulders in its lazy caress. I didn't dare move out too far;

I could still drown. I scoffed at my own timidity, and for the next hour, I taught myself how to float, and how to swim like a dog. I felt empowered. Enlightened. The burden of the nix was finally gone. When I eased myself from the pool, I held within my chest a sense of satisfaction.

Standing on the bank, arms akimbo, I glared down at the pool. "You don't scare me anymore. You were never real."

From that day forward, I couldn't wait to get to the pool by the lake. I taught myself how to swim, not satisfied until my strokes were strong and my kicks churned the water into a frothy foam. All those years of worry evaporated. My smile came easier, my laugh freer.

My parents noticed my altered mood. They dared to hope all would be well. And as my swimming became stronger, I hoped so, too. Living by deceit became my only regret, for I didn't have the heart to tell my parents what I'd done. On more than one occasion, my mother eyed me with alarm when I came home with my clothes smelling of lake water. She never said a word, so I never had to lie…or tell her that the tale of the nix was just that–a make-believe story caused by my father's over-active mind.

In the summer of my seventeenth year, I went to town on a special occasion. Gordie was to marry. I could as much ignore the event as I could my own foot. I had, to my surprise, successfully avoided thinking of Nari for nearly two years. And why not? I'd found peace with myself at last. I'd learned many trades, deepened my relationship with my parents and torn myself free of the curse. I was overjoyed to find that my doom was no longer inevitable.

Yet, a nagging sense that my time of peace had

finally come to an end settled over me.

When my family reached the chapel, I slipped in after my parents, hoping to avoid the stares of the villagers.

No such luck. A restless wait had settled over the chapel, and as soon as I sat, the man in front of us turned and smiled. "'Tis good to see you, lad. You've been out of sight for so long, I feared the nix had finally come and claimed you."

A loud snicker and snort followed his seemingly innocent interest as he winked at one of his friends sitting close by. For some, the superstition held an underlying jest. Surely if the tale were real, the nix would have claimed her prize. The nix's tale had lost the worst of its bite, and in recent years, my family suffered looks of ridicule along with those of fear. I wanted nothing more than to sink down and pray this would all be over so I could go back into hiding.

Never one to take offense, my father quickly corrected the man. "We thank God for his blessings and his help in allowing Ryne to avoid such a catastrophe. It's a certainty the nix still awaits him in the mist. But we have trained him well to stay clear of the water."

He made me sound as if I were his favorite hunting dog. "Father, please," I whispered. "This is not the time."

"He is right," my mother said. Her face suddenly flared to life at the entry of the bride. At that moment, all the women nudged their men and the buzz of boredom quieted.

As I watched the ceremony, I became aware of Gordie's pale face and shaking hands. His bride, a girl from a village to the west, couldn't stop casting loving looks at him from beneath her circlet of flowers.

"Is she not lovely?" my mother murmured in a

voice gooey with sentiment.

"Gordie looks ill," I whispered back as the couple faced the crowd, now husband and wife.

"And so do all grooms, for to take a wife is no small matter," my father inserted.

"Then why marry if it is such a burden?"

"But a more pleasant burden I have yet to find," my father quipped back.

My mother shushed us as the couple passed on their way out of the chapel. "He looks grand. A handsome groom for a pretty bride."

My father and I exchanged a quick look over the romantic notions of my mother. "To you," he said, "all grooms are handsome and all brides pretty."

"True. But Gordie and his love are especially grand," she said as we moved forward, awaiting our turn to follow the bride and groom from the building.

As we stood in the mesh of people, I caught a glimpse of a female out of the corner of my eye. A real beauty. When I turned to get a better look, she had disappeared. I bent and whispered in my mother's ear. "There are many who have traveled from the bride's village to be here."

"She must be well loved."

If I married, it may very well draw a crowd, but only because my family was an oddity and I the oddest male amongst a sparse collection of youth.

Once outside, the celebration began with music and dancing and mountains of food. It didn't take long for the drink to loosen tongues and the tall tales to flow. My father's exaggerated account of the nix soon became the favorite. I tolerated the stares and the whispers as the locals told the visitors all about my forthcoming doom.

Like a good son, I made my rounds, reacquainting

myself with those who'd thought I'd died and meeting those who believed I soon would. I passed a group of women—those of our village as well as the bride's—hovering near the table laden with sweet cakes, and I heard Gordie's step-mother say with surprise, "Him? Ryne, the stonemason's son?"

I acted as if I heard not a word, though how one could miss her strident tones was a mystery, and I stalled over my choice to hear more.

"Oh, dear," she said in a dramatic whisper. "Not Ryne. His family is…special, and as poor as the soil on the fen. The father is a good man, quite skilled in fact, but he has a fanciful nature, and you wouldn't want that passed down the family tree. And if the tale of the nix is true, what daughter would thank her mother over that match? I'm sure a girl can do much better than him."

I grunted, selected a nice carrot cake, and moved on. I guess I need not worry about attracting a wife. I took a big bite, not able to enjoy its sweetness as her words replayed in my head at a distracting din. So, I was no favor. I tried to feel offended, but I couldn't. My parents, in their worry over my safety, had made sure I was no prize. I glanced over at them, so unaware of the damage they had caused. I loved them, but…

My gaze slid away and touched on the girl I'd seen in the chapel. An exceptionally beautiful girl. And I was not the only one to notice. I took a big bite of the sweet cake and chewed. Tait had cozied up to her and was literally falling all over himself to charm her into his capable arms. The girl barely seemed to notice him. Smart girl. She looked distracted; her gaze flighty as it slashed through the crowd, and then onto me.

Our eyes met and held. In the waning light, I could not see if hers were blue or brown, but they turned up at the outside edges just like ...

I choked.

"Nari?"

She looked different. Not at all like I expected.

"I see you found her," Gordie whispered in my ear after he'd snuck up on me. The color had returned to his cheeks, and he gazed proudly over at his little sister. "Who would have thought my aunt capable of making a lady out of a lad, but she did."

My gaze stabbed Tait in the back. "What is *he* doing cooing over your little sister?" I looked back at her and noticed a decided change in her demeanor. Where before she had ignored Tait, now she batted her eyelashes and made silly faces that encouraged his suit. "Will you look at her? How can she forget how much she hates him?"

"People change. You did."

"Not Nari. She hates Tait. She always has and always will."

"Well then," Gordie said with a smile, "I guess you had best get over there and remind her who Tait is."

6

Cobalt Eyes Beneath Dark Skies

I knew who Tait was. He was the one all the girls swooned over. But he was also the one who'd tormented Nari when we were young—the last to agree to let her stay, and the first to tell her to go home. How could she forget? It was embarrassing...humiliating the way she fawned over him. Worse, I wanted to be him. I wanted her to look at me with adoration. I wanted her quick touches and soft laughs. Evil as it sounded, I wanted the ground to open up and swallow Tait whole, and for me to take his place.

I still wanted Nari. More than ever. And this time I wasn't scared to let her know it. I was, as Gordie pointed out, a changed man.

I threw the remaining carrot cake to the ground and headed toward the pair. Tait had his back to me, so it wasn't terribly difficult to slip around him and take Nari's hand in mine.

"Excuse us," I said to the rogue, though I looked squarely into Nari's cobalt blue eyes, which had widened at my touch. Without missing a beat, or waiting for Tait to agree, I pulled her behind me, and miracles of miracles, she followed without a sound of protest. I quickly led her around the side of the house, and when we were out of sight, I pulled her into my arms and kissed her.

Sugary lips, soft skin and the sweet smell of her skin assailed me. I was undone. A slave to her. My best friend. Her fingers clasped the front of my shirt, and I pulled her closer. Why had I ever sent her away from me? I'd been a brainless dolt. A child. But a child no longer. If any man were to touch her, it would be me, and only me.

Slowly we pulled apart, her name on my lips interrupted by a sharp slap to my cheek. I threw my eyes open and put a hand to my stinging skin. When I looked down, it was into Nari's surprisingly furious features. We had experienced the most wondrous kiss and she was mad? Incomprehensible. "What did you do that for?"

Her fists pummeled my chest before I could jump out of reach. When I managed to break free, I stood apart from her, baffled by her unexpected attack. She stared at me, her body stiff and unyielding as she screamed, "What is wrong with you? Do you think, after all these years, you can just come and kiss me without even a polite greeting?"

"But…" I motioned to the front of the house like an idiot, "you came along…"

"I thought you were finally going to apologize."

What was she talking about? "Apologize? For what? We've not seen each other in nearly two years."

I quickly stepped back as the heat of a long stoked fire burst from her soft lips. "You broke my heart. You were my best friend and you ran away."

Oh, right. That. I scrambled to explain my behavior. "I was…confused."

"About what?" she asked, stepping closer.

I matched each of her forward steps with a backward one of my own, keeping a good distance between us. "You changed. You were a girl. I didn't understand what had happened, or why I'd suddenly noticed when the day before I hadn't."

She stalked me around the back yard. "Are you telling me you forgot I was a girl, and the day you remembered, you ran?"

The blaze in her heart had turned to an inferno and her arms flailed wildly as she continued her advance.

"Are you going to hit me again?" I was a little worried about that because my cheek really hurt.

She stopped chasing me, and a look of regret flittered across her face. "No."

I took a step closer. "Nari, must we argue? It was two years ago. Neither of us are the same person."

"Two years," she repeated.

I dared to hope. "That's right. Two years."

Her foot suddenly came out and slammed in to my shin. "And they've been the most awful two years of my life. I want an apology."

Pain lanced up my leg and I hobbled back, rubbing the ache away as I shot her a heated glare. "That hurt."

"Not as badly as you hurt me."

"You can't keep it against me. I was just a lad."

"Apologize," she yelled in a threatening voice.

I'd never seen that exact shade of purplish-red on a woman's face before. It terrified me.

"I'm sorry," I yelled back.

"That's not good enough," she raged, her beautiful face flushed even brighter with anger. "You were the only one who treated me like I mattered. When you were around, I wasn't invisible. Don't you get it? When you rejected me, I wanted to die."

Her eyes grew bright with unshed tears. "Nay, I nearly did."

If the heat coming off her could kill, I'd be roasted welldone.

I deserved no less fate.

I had abandoned her because I'd been afraid of growing up. How could she have known the fear that plagued me? She hadn't done anything wrong. I didn't want to think what must have gone through her mind when I'd deserted her so cruelly. Guilt washed over me as I looked into her face. "You're right. It's not good enough. I'm sorry I hurt you, Nari. I was young and stupid and I don't deserve your forgiveness, but I'm asking, no, I'm begging you." I dropped to my knees in front of her, unmindful of how I looked. "Will you forgive me?"

A crowd had gathered to watch, drawn no doubt, by our yelling. Nari cast a dubious glance at me. "So, you want me to forgive you?"

"Please," I said in my most fervent voice. "Forgive me."

"You were my best friend." The whispered confession almost broke my heart.

"I still am. I promise. I'm sorry."

She bit her lip in indecision. I'd never felt so horrible or so nervous. The sun had set and torchlight caused the highlights in her hair to dance. Her skin shone like butter and cream and I ached just looking at her. "Please, Nari. Forgive me."

She stepped closer. "Ryne," she said in a soft husky voice. My name sounded so sweet on her lips.

My heart lifted. "Yes?"

She took another step closer.

"Watch it, lad," someone yelled.

Her fist shot out and the next thing I knew, I was laid flat on the ground and sporting an aching jaw. Her aim was accurate as always and stung just as much. I glanced up into Nari's spitting cobalt blue eyes. "What did you do that for?"

"You are the stupidest boy I have ever met."

With that, she turned and stomped away amidst the laughter of the crowd.

Gordie approached and held out his hand. Holding my sore jaw with one hand, I clasped his with the other and let him help me stand. As the crowd slowly dispersed, Gordie critiqued my performance. "Good show of regret, but I think you should've kissed her first."

"I did."

Tait appeared at Gordie's shoulder, his ever-present grin causing my jaw to tighten. "Then you mustn't have done it right. Poor Ryne. To be known as a bad kisser is almost as bad as being known as a sad ending to a faery tale. Speaking of tales, how's the nix in the lake?"

"Shut up, Tait."

Before I lost all control, I stormed away to coddle my wounded pride in peace.

And then I did a very stupid thing.

I went to the pool.

The night was thick, but held a robust moon, which threw down silver slashes of light that cut into the pool's murky water. I'd never seen a moon such as this, the way it lit the night like a mighty beacon, nor felt the depth of my soul so keenly. Melancholy overtook me and I stripped down to only my trews and dove into the pond, letting the water soothe my aching muscles and clear my head.

The water slid against my skin. A feeling of buoyant freedom engulfed me. I dove and swam, spanning the pool several times until I moved to the waterfall. On a previous visit, I'd found a ledge just behind the falling water. I dove beneath the churning surface and resurfaced behind the silvery veil. I shook the excess water off my hair and tried to peer through the break in the falling water.

At one point, I thought I saw someone. I waited, but the vision did not return. As my body cooled, I thought of what I must do. I had to speak with Nari. She would be leaving for her aunt's house soon. I couldn't leave our last moment together laden with memories of an argument.

Standing, I dove back into the water and resurfaced just beyond the bubbling waters near the falls. The mists were rolling in from the lake. Soon they would engulf far inland like a wet blanket, and disappear when the sun touched the horizon. There was no finer sight than seeing the sun's first finger of life touch the low mist golden white. Nari would love the sight.

As I swam toward the bank, something grazed my leg. I jerked to a stop. Treading water, I looked around me, trying to see into the pool's murky depths. For all the times I'd gone swimming here, I'd never felt any fish so much as nibble on my baby toe.

Again something grazed my leg, and I instinctively kicked out. Without hesitating, I darted toward the bank. The sensation that something unseen and dangerous lurked in the water spurred me on. As soon as I touched the bank, I vaulted out of the water, but not before I heard the rip of my trews and felt a sharp scratch along the length of my calf as I yanked my leg out.

I whipped myself around, my skin slick, my trews slashed and sodden and molded to my lower body. I peered into the water. The silver light that had guided me was gone, leaving the pool a blackened hole that could just as easily be filled with tar as it was with water.

I stood shivering in the night as the mist edged further along the edge of the pool. The moon gave a last flicker of light, revealing the water's surface and an old tree branch bobbing near where I'd climbed from the water. I released my breath, unaware I'd been holding it until then.

"A branch. Just a branch." No nix had come to drag me to her underwater domain.

It disturbed me to think in some corner of my brain, I could still believed my parent's tale. I was no better than they. I let out a ragged laugh. "I'm a fool." A fool to believe a foolish faerytale.

I collected the rest of my clothes and walked away, feeling the bloody scratch on my calf burn as I did.

7

 A Most Stubborn Girl

On my return from my swim, I was waylaid on my trek home. As a favored friend of the groom's, I was enlisted to help clean up the commons. Empty kegs were hauled back to the pub, chairs were hefted back into their respective houses, and men were supported back to their beds. All-in-all, it was backbreaking work. While I rested from helping old man Tiller limp—though it was really a stagger—to his house, I overheard Nari's father and the new wife.

"You must rest now, husband," she said, patting him on the arm. "No one will mind. You have a long journey on the morrow, and I'll need you home by week's end."

Nari's father cleared his throat. "There will be no journey."

The new wife suddenly grew tense and her eyes latched onto her husband.

He shrugged off her alarm. "Nari will not be returning to her aunt's house. Her training is complete."

Crickets could be heard in the silence that followed that announcement, for he was not a man conditioned toward conflict. He let his wife have what she willed so long as she saw to the house, fed him and left him in peace. But the new wife regained her voice soon enough. "Surely you realize it is unfair to assume such a conclusion this soon?"

He glanced away. "I never thought I'd miss her, but I do. She stays."

Unused to him giving orders, she stuttered. "B-but…"

Panic covered the new wife's face. "It is best to finish the job than to leave it half done. Even you must see the folly of trying to give away a half-trained wife."

Nari's father slanted an exhausted look toward her. "Stop your fretting, woman. What you could not accomplish is where my sister has excelled. Nari is all that a young woman should be, and I have every confidence she will be of great use to you." With that, he walked away.

The new wife was rarely one to be put off. "And if your confidence is misplaced," her displeasure railed against him, "a great burden. Left unmarried, she will drain our monies until there is none left."

A ray of hope lightened my chest. I cared little if the new wife was pleased or not, her husband's decision favored me, for it gave me a fighting chance to secure Nari's forgiveness…and maybe a tiny speck of her love. Though bruised and frustrated, I was suddenly energized in my campaign to win Nari.

The day after the wedding, I rose early and set out for Nari's home. I passed Gordie's new house, and everyone else's in the village, before I came to a stop outside a charming thatched cottage. I had to hand it to the new wife. Over the years, she had managed to work her magic on the dilapidated little cottage, making a pretty purse out of a sow's ear. Morning glories draped the flowerbeds while climbing roses edged up the sides of the house, dripping red, and pink and white along the eaves. A fine, full kitchen garden had been planted out back and improvements to the overall construction to the place had been done—namely by myself and my father.

I waited in the darkness of the morning, rehearsing what I would say to Nari. I waited until the sun sprang from its long night's rest to cast the first yellow vines of light along the streets. Not long after, a light in the window flickered brightly, and I straightened from my squatting position at the corner of the house across the lane.

I couldn't move.

I just stood there, staring at the house as the village slowly awoke. As the dairyman went house to house, leaving the morning jugs beside each door. As the women rose to make a hearty breakfast for their families. As the men left for another day of labor. A young boy came and handed a letter to the new wife. Its contents making her squeal with delight. "You see here?" she crowed. "I didn't imagine it." And the door shut on her excitement.

Through it all, I was a sad piece of work, standing in the shadows there like a forgotten, ill-loved dog.

I avoided Nari's father as he left the house, hiding like a cornered rat, terrified he'd see me. I shouldn't have worried. He was too busy to mind the idiot hunkering in the shadows.

Not so everyone.

"Ryne, is that you skulking about over there?" a crusty, thick voice shouted.

My gaze shot to old widow Jens scuffling down the

alleyway. Her steps were so slow, and she so slight, it was a wonder the wind didn't knock her over before she was able to put her foot down. Within one hand, she held a basket and in the other a stout walking stick. As she peered over at me, I could hardly deny it was not I, for everyone knew everyone here.

She answered her own question before I could. "Yes, it's you. Strange thing last night. Why would you yell at poor Nari, and her back for only a few days? Can't say as your mother is pleased with your manners. That's why you're here. Come to make things right. Well, get on with you," she said, close enough now to swat me with her cane. "You know the way and the how to."

With my throat too constricted to say anything, I only nodded as I endured the prod of her stick. Under the widow's watchful stare, I stepped up to the door and gave it a quick rap. I glanced back, and she gave me a satisfied nod. At the sound of footsteps from within, I faced the door and swallowed rapidly in an effort to lubricate my dry throat.

The door sprang open to reveal the new wife wearing a wide smile on her face and dressed in her best finery. One look at me and her smile disappeared. "What do you want?"

"I'd...I'd like to speak with Nari, if you don't mind." And then, in a brilliant show of afterthought, I tacked on, "Ma'am."

Her nose twitched with disgust, completely unimpressed. "She isn't in."

How was that possible? I'd been staring at the house since before dawn. "May I ask where she is?"

"You may not." She took a step forward, forcing me back as she waved her hand holding the letter that had been delivered that morning. "You hie yourself somewhere else. Nari has a suitor coming today to talk of an arrangement, and if he sees you hanging about, no telling what he'll think of us."

"Someone wants to marry Nari?" Word of her staying had traveled fast. Though I heard correctly, I couldn't quite believe her.

"I'm as shocked as you, but that's what he states. 'As pretty a wife as I'll likely get,' he says. And I'm right glad to hear it. A godsend, he is." She looked up and down the street, her gaze piercing the shadows for any sign of her prey before returning to me. "Away with you, now," she hissed, and made to close the door, but I stopped her.

"Who?"

She looked from my hand on the door to me, and it was clear she was not pleased. "No one you would know."

"Does her father know of your plan?"

"What impudence," she bristled like a porcupine. "Of course he knows."

"Does Nari?"

She blustered and gurgled and looked ready to erupt. "I'll not say another word to you, young man. Be gone or I'll fetch my husband to throw you away."

With a hefty shove, she closed the door, leaving me to stare thoughtfully at the solid panel. Nari couldn't know. But what if she did? Was that why she had been so ill-disposed toward me last night?

"No," I said as I backed away. "She wouldn't marry a stranger."

"And who says he's a stranger?" said the old widow.

I whipped my head toward the forgotten widow and blinked. "Nari can't marry. She promised me she wouldn't."

The old woman snorted and shook her head. "A young girl's promise is a worthless vow. Easily made, easily broken."

But Nari was not like other girls. We had a blood pact...an understanding...the two of us, forever. She would never marry just anyone. As I stood in the brightness of a clear morning, the world turned gray, all the joy leeched from it by one word.

Married.

I spun on my heels and ran.

"It's time, you know," the widow Jens yelled after me. "If left on the shelf too long, her beauty will grow stale, and then where will she be?"

I ran until I came to a newly built cottage, stopping only when I collided with the stout door. I pounded on it as if I were a hare being chased by wolves. I would not let up, banging until the door was jerked open from beneath my fist.

Gordie, his trews riding low on his hips and his chest bare to the cool morning air, shot an irritated look at me and rasped, "You dare to knock on my door on my wedding night?"

"It's morning."

He pushed his hand through his tousled hair and peered past me, a look of surprise on his face. "So it is."

"Who is it?" a young, sweet voice called from within.

"Just the village idiot come to beg for a hot bun, my love. I'll be just a moment." He stepped outside and closed the door, then faced me. Displeasure creased his brow. "This had better be good, Ryne. The next five seconds of your life depends on it."

"What do you know about a man coming to wed Nari?"

Gordie put his hands on his hips and laughed. When he saw I was serious, he cocked his head questioningly at me. "Have you been drinking?"

"I'm serious. Your stepmother said some man is coming to make arrangements to marry her."

"Well, he'll not get far. Nari swears she'll have no one."

"Do you think your stepmother would promise Nari without her permission?"

Gordie thought for a moment. "That would be a bold move, but–oh bloody hell, she would. Her one real challenge has been to see us out of her house. And now that Nari is back…well, she'll want to get her out for good."

Alarm gripped me. I grabbed Gordie's shoulders. "I'll find Nari."

"I'll find my father," he replied.

We broke away, each running in the opposite direction. I didn't know where to look. I hunted the forest in a haphazard pattern, panic skewing my search. Just by chance, I found myself beneath the tree we had used to lie in wait for our victims. And just by chance, I glanced up.

Nari, dressed in one of Gordie's old trews and a shirt, stared down at me. I couldn't believe my eyes. "Nari?"

She curled her bare feet under her as if she were embarrassed to be caught up a tree. "Hello, Ryne."

"What are you doing up there?"

"I like the view."

I turned, but all I could see were trees and trees and more trees. I quickly kicked off my shoes and climbed up. It had been a few years since I'd been up this particular tree, and to my surprise, all the handholds and footholds remained. When I got to her branch, I scooted out beside her.

She cast me a nervous look, but didn't say anything. I looked out to where she had been staring and I could see through the break in the trees the sparkling waters of the lake and my house.

"It's a lovely view," she said.

"It is," I agreed, seeing once again why my mother loved her house on the lake. "Why did I never notice it before?"

A shy smile touched her lips. "You were always looking down, ready to spit…or worse."

I smiled back, drinking in the way the wind gently blew her hair against her cheek. "I guess so. I never knew you weren't doing the same."

"I usually was. I only saw it once you left. I'd sit here for hours praying you'd come back."

My smile faded and a tightness entered my throat. "I'm so sorry, Nari. Please believe me. I was being thick. A complete ass."

"I'll not argue with you there." She slid a curious look at me. "Why are you here?"

"I was looking for you. I went to your house, to find you, and your stepmother said a man was coming."

She looked blankly at me. "And?"

"And that he would be making an offer for you."

She blinked, and her gaze shifted away. "Did she say who?"

That was not the reaction I expected. "You don't sound surprised. You can't be thinking of marrying?"

"Why not? Gordie's wife is not even a year older than me."

I watched her swing from the limb and climb down as quick as when she was just a lad. I couldn't have heard her correctly. I followed her down, and once on the ground, I faced her. "You cannot get married."

"What?"

"You cannot." She was mine. We belonged together. The day of our pact sat so clearly in my mind. "What of this?" I said and held out my hand where a small scar had formed across the palm, an exact replica of the one on hers.

She pushed my hand away. "Be serious."

"I am."

"Well then, you do not remember well, for what I remember is saying exactly what we all vowed never to do, and trust me, I am the only one of you lot who will never break that vow."

She spoke of the pact we all made, though I spoke of ours. Yet even then she lied. "How can you say that?" I pointed up the tree in an effort to bring her memory to the oh-so-recent past. "You just admitted you've been thinking of marrying."

She let loose a deep laugh. It reminded me of times past, and I felt some hope. "I vowed what you did, Ryne. Never to marry a *girl*, and I can honestly say, I plan on keeping that vow."

"But…you *cannot* marry him." I heard the whine in my voice, and to my utter disgust, I couldn't stop it.

"Cannot? You lost the right to tell me what to do long ago, Ryne. I do what I want now." She turned, her face set, her shoulders squared, and started down the road.

I'd never felt so sick in my life as when I watched her proudly walk away.

8

Without

The sickness which had settled in the pit of my stomach didn't last long. Nari couldn't marry some stranger. This was a poor joke. Punishment for my behavior of last night. She was always one for big talk. I raced after her, catching up once we neared the village.

Without looking at me, she said, "Go away, Ryne. This is none of your business."

"Cannot a man walk where he will?"

An unpleasant smile cracked her lips. "Oh, so you are a man now?"

"I am what you see," I said, holding out my arms, begging her to take a good look.

She did, her gaze sweeping me up and down. "Well, then ..." she said, not agreeing or disagreeing. "You may not walk where you will if your walk is in the same direction I take."

I dropped my arms. "Sadly for you, I believe it is."

I ignored her heated glare and continued on my journey of discovery, half teasing, half terrified. "Tell me, have you even met your future husband?"

I saw the muscle in her jaw tighten, and then relax. With a forced air of cheer, she said, "Has anyone truly met anyone?"

I knew her game. "So," I said with a smile, "this does come as a surprise. Poor Nari."

"Do not dare pity me. I have had *several* men of late who have voiced interest in me."

I made of show of looking around. "And where might they be? Hiding in the bushes readying themselves to snatch you from your family? Come fellows," I called. "Have you not heard? Her stepmother will gladly give her away."

She smacked me in the stomach, causing a loud woof to escape me and snarled, "I have refused them all."

After recovering from the hit, I cast her a quizzical look. "Why?"

Her eye slanted toward me before she raised her nose in the air. "They had the unfortunate ability to remind me of you."

"I see." She meant it meanly, but I took it to mean something different. "Why settle for an imitation when the original is what you want. Very perceptive of you."

She suddenly stopped and began to look around. I frowned. "Have you lost something?"

"Not yet, but my breakfast is soon to come forth, and I'm looking for a bush to be sick on." After throwing me an angry glance meant to put me in my place, she quickened her steps, giving me a quick backward glance.

My lips twitched against a coming smile. Cheeky girl. I chased her as was her want. Soon, the village welcomed us, and seeing as we were nearly trotting down the lane, her house loomed quickly before us. I had to do something before she made the worst mistake of her life…and mine.

Mere steps from her front door, I stood my ground. "Nari," I yelled, stopping her in her place. She didn't turn, but held her back in rigid defense against me. I wouldn't be put off.

"Please. I know you are angry with me. You have every right. I behaved like a...a stupid, half-brained pig. But you must know how you terrify me. You have since the day I realized you meant more to me than anyone else. That is a terrifying thought for a lad. But not anymore. If I would have been given one scrap of hope that you loved me, I would have cured this constant ache you have plunged me into long ago."

She twirled around and pinned me with her dark blue stare. Her cheeks flared scarlet and her mouth twisted as she spoke. "And how would you have done that?"

How would I?

A frown creased my brow and into my mind. Indeed, how would I?

I quickly sought the cure for this horrible ailment, and when it presented itself to me, it was as if the answer came straight from God. "I am told that to get over a fear you must look it straight in the eye."

"Stop saying that you fear me. It's—"

Before I lost my nerve, I swooped down and kissed her. This was no sweet peck. It was the kiss of the desperate, the lost, the hopeful. Our breaths melded, our hearts combined. I pulled her tightly to me and poured every ounce of my being into that kiss. I felt her respond, but I dared not hope. She had a wily nature. When our lips parted, I dared not open my eyes, afraid of the condemnation that awaited me.

"Do not ask for my regret," was all I could mutter, still holding her securely against my chest. I placed my chin on her head, fighting the sick feeling that washed over my skin. "Without you, I…bloody hell. I just cannot see you married. You are mine. You and me together, forever. Do you truly not remember?"

Slowly, she pulled away, her fingers trailing against my chest where she had placed her open palms to ward me off. Yet something in her touch felt more like a caress. I opened my eyes to find a soft smile on her face. She tipped her head back, her eyes twinkling merrily.

I tensed. Was this another of her tricks? Should I push her away to save my body further harm?

Her tongue dashed against her pink lips as one of her fingers twirled against my chest. "I do remember. But if you deny me marriage, then you put us in a sad state indeed, for I see myself quite happily married. To you."

"Me?" I mouthed, as if saying it aloud would bring about disaster.

True to form, she slammed her fist into my chest before she threw her arms around me and planted her lips quite firmly to mine. The soft rosebud mouth branded me forever as hers, leaching all energy from me until my legs felt more skin than bone. I'd died and gone to heaven.

"Nari!" The shrill sound of the demented tore us apart. Gasping, we faced the new wife seething before us in all her outrage. A man, clearly in possession of some wealth yet with the unfortunate luck to be of round stature, broad face and stubby appendages, stood beside her, glaring bug-eyed at me. His lip curled as his gaze turned to Nari.

I clutched for the sanity that seemed to have deserted me. Mine. Mine. Mine. That was the litany that coursed through my veins. I would squash this pathetic toad that stood in the way of my happiness. My fingers sought hers and once found, entwined like a vine not easily pulled from its mooring and tugged her behind me. If he wanted her, he would have to go through me.

"Is this what I am to claim as my wife?" the man croaked. "A woman of easy conquest? I would have given her everything, and you a goodly endowment for your old age. Providence has surely smiled down on me. I shan't trouble myself over her a moment longer."

The new wife's face paled at the thought of such a fortune and its sudden evaporation. Her lips flapped soundlessly like a land-bound trout. "P-p-please," she finally said, "Oh sir, please do not be rash. It is all the boy's fault. He is a scoundrel at best."

The man pushed his way to the lane, and without a backward glance, brandished his rolling gait as a farmer would a plow, cutting a wide furrow through the villagers as he made haste to leave. Hurrying quickly toward us, Gordie and his father were forced to jump out of the man's way.

"Husband, husband," the new wife screeched, waving her arms and pointing after the furious man. "Do something."

Nari's father glanced after the man and shrugged from across the lane. "What am I to do?"

"He is getting away. As you dawdle, our future son-in-law escapes."

We all stared after the poor rich man and watched as he pushed his way through, knocking over a cart of produce and pushing aside the old widow, who raised her cane and plied it toward his head. Unfortunately, she was too late and he moved on without injury. I was not upset at her failure, for such a knock on the head could have put some sense into him and shown him the prize he was so eager to leave, and one I was so eager to take from him.

Nari's father crossed his arms over his chest and glowered after the man. "Then I say godspeed to him, wife. By his manners, he is not a man I would have enjoyed as a son-in-law."

The new wife wiggled her fingers toward the end of the lane as if that alone would call the toad back. Her mouth flapped open, lips quivering against the forthcoming fit of temper. "B-b-b-b..."

With an amazing ability to ignore the oncoming storm of tears and howls, Nari's father turned to his son. "A fine morning this is, eh Gordie?"

Still gazing down the lane with a smug smile on his face, Gordie replied, "None finer."

"And your wife? Does she appreciate this morn?"

"My wife?" He turned a blank gaze on his father and then his face lit with horror. "My wife." He whirled around and ran down the lane like a raw-boned lad toward his new house and his hopefully still starry-eyed wife.

Nari's father turned toward me and focused on my hand earnestly clutching his daughter's. That gaze clearly stated he would be more than happy to break every bone in my body if I didn't disengage myself from his daughter immediately. Like a well-trained dog, I ripped my fingers from hers and scuttered back a healthy distance. "Good morn to you, sir. I'll just be on my way."

I shot a meaningful glance at Nari, but she found herself trying to cut off the new wife's tantrum at losing a wealthy son-in-law by way of ushering her into the house, a job too large for her to notice my impending danger. With a quick bow to the man, I shot down the lane with all my bones unbroken, but more importantly with the taste of Nari still on my lips, the tingling brand of her hand against mine, and the hope that the curse I'd lived under all these years would finally be over.

9

Not That Stupid

Bliss. My life, once a sad collection of hours in a day, exploded into a never-ending moment of pure bliss. For the next two months, Nari and I spent every free moment together. We returned to the familiarity of our youth with amazing ease. We laughed. We teased. We remembered whispered secrets and life and death vows. One day, I snuck up on Nari as she was pegging out the laundry.

"Practicing for the future?" came my quick whisper before I pulled away.

We were careful to appear as friends in public, but the strain of not touching her was beginning to take its toll.

She spun around and smiled. "A woman does not need to practice. She is born with a ladle in one hand and a laundry peg in the other."

"How very…practical." I gazed around. "Home alone?"

"Asked the wolf to the woman." She cast me a challenging glance. "I am."

A thrill raced through me. I immediately grabbed her hand and pulled her in for a kiss. When we pulled apart, I rasped thickly, "Finish your chores."

The rest of the laundry was pegged, though not nearly as neatly as before, and we scurried away.

I took her to the lake to walk along the shore. It was one of the few places I was certain we could be alone, for most were afraid to draw too near. We rested in a small copse of trees where the lap and pull of the water sounded behind me. Nari sat on a felled tree, her gaze wide and uncertain. "I still cannot believe it. To see you so near the lake. It feels wrong. Dangerous."

"Why? I live just past those trees," I said pointing toward the tight jumble of trunks and branches. "On a windy day, my back door gets wet with lake water. The lake and I are familiar foes, and yet we share a familiar secret, one you will never guess."

Interest flared behind her intense gaze, for Nari loved a good secret. I held out my hand and she grabbed hold. With a light tug, I pulled her close and began a slow move backwards. "There is much you don't know about me."

She scoffed at the idea and ran her free hand up my chest teasingly, confident in her knowledge. "I doubt that."

"It is a daring secret no one else knows."

I felt her squirm with anticipation. Bending low, I whispered in her ear. "I can swim."

She reared back and yanked me still. "You lie."

I swept her into my arms and twirled her in a circle. She laughed and yelled for me to put her down. I did. Right into the lake.

She yelped as the water lapped at her dress, and she threw a startled gaze up at me. I pulled my shirt off and tossed it on the dry shore. She cocked her head and merriment colored her voice, "What are you about?"

"Proof."

Her smile waned. "Proof of what?"

I backed away, the water slipping over my feet, past my ankles and up my calves. "That I can swim."

In the distance dark clouds began to form. Neither of us paid much attention as Nari took my hand and tugged me back to shore. "Oh no you don't. You need not prove anything to me. If you say you can swim, I believe you. If you say you wish to be a hoary old billy goat... well, that is very believable, too."

I ducked my head and butted her until she came up against the fallen tree. She placed her hand on the crown of my head and laughed. "I yield. What would you have of me?"

"A kiss," I said, though I wanted far more.

She pulled my face close, wrapped her arms around my neck and with a sigh, pressed her lips to mine. An ache of longing speared through me. I tugged her close, fitting her as tightly against my chest as I could and bent her backwards until we dangled over the edge of the tree. A squeal of alarm rose in her throat, but there was no fear in her eyes. For good measure I twisted and we fell, landing softly on the ground with her atop me and not once loosing her lips. I held her face in my hands glorying in the touch of her soft skin. Never would not let her go.

We stayed in the small shelter of trees and brush, protected from the rising wind and the spray of turbulent water. Her lips teased my skin, leaving a trail of heat wherever they touched. I didn't think my heart could stand such torture, but it seemed quite capable of accepting the punishment and actually wanted more.

Placing my forehead to hers, I drew in a jagged breath.

"Is aught wrong," she whispered her concern.

"Never. It's just…"

Our hands were clasped, and I drew them down and flattened her palm to my chest. I lifted my gaze to hers. "Do you see what you do to me?"

Her face softened and as we stared into each other's eyes, she placed my hand to her chest directly over her heart. It merrily tripped along matching my pulse beat for beat. The tip of her tongue darted over her lips before a shy smile formed. "I know exactly how you feel."

My love for her had never been greater. As we explored each other, the trust she offered, the love she gave to me, a doomed man, humbled me. I wished fervently that time would stand still. That today would always be and tomorrow would never come. Yet all too soon our moment ended. The stomp of feet and the boom of a male's voice interrupted us.

"Nari."

The call broke through the haze of my longing and I pulled away. Nari tried to pull me back, but I refused and peered through the brush. "Someone calls for you."

Her name ripped against the wind, again and again. She struggled to a sitting position, never looking lovelier with her hair mussed and her lips a burnished pink. I wanted to pull her to me and burrow further into the brush where we could hide from the world that threatened to pull us apart, but I knew my wishes were not to be.

She turned toward me and frowned. "I-I think it's Tait. He visits nearly every week now."

"I thought you told him to go away?"

"I did, but you know him. He doesn't listen well."

He must have heard us talking, for the next thing we knew, he poked his head between the trees and scowled down at us. "What are you doing?"

The condemnation in his voice was not lost on me. I rose and faced him. "Nothing that concerns you."

Tait forced himself into our haven and pulled Nari to her feet. She yanked her hands free, and he watched as she straightened her clothes and smoothed her hair. "Your parents are worried sick. You've been gone far too long."

Nari cast him a suspicious look and stepped closer to me. "I highly doubt that."

Tait stepped closer and a haggard whisper tore from his throat. "Don't do this, Nari. He's not worth it. He'll never be able to care for you like..." He hesitated.

"You?" she sneered. "As if I would have you."

His face darkened. "People are talking."

"I care not."

"Think of your family."

She entwined her fingers defiantly between mine.

The wind brought the sound of her name again. It was Gordie. Nari glanced up at me in surprise.

"See?" Tait pounced on her concern. "They are worried. A storm is rising and you were nowhere to be found."

"Go," I said, and gave her a little nudge.

Reluctantly, she let go, and with a careless hand, she pushed by Tait.

When she was gone, he turned on me, his chest heaving with suppressed rage. "She's too good for you. She deserves far more than what you could ever offer, so I'm going to say this only once. Let her be. Disappear. It's your fate, Ryne. Your time on earth is numbered."

I stepped closer to him. "Is that a threat?"

"It's the truth." With one last hate-filled look, he left.

The wind that only a moment before had whipped through the treetops grew still. The waves gentled. Not me. I stood with hands balled into fists at my side trembling with rage. I picked up a few flat stones and whipped them out over the water. One. Two. Three skips until the waves gobbled up the first rock. I glanced in the direction Tait had gone, turning the second stone in my fingers. "She's too good for you, too."

With a snap of my wrist the stone zipped across the water. One. Two.

I turned, not bothering to see its final skip as I pushed my way from the shelter of the trees. I would not be scared off. Nari was mine.

A few days later we climbed our tree, and I settled with my back against the trunk and Nari leaning against my chest. Even the simplest contact between us stoked the fires of my desire. Tait's threats held no sway over me, for there was no doubt in my mind. Nari and I were meant for each other. Even when we were apart, our hearts never wandered far. Ours was a love that had grown despite the stubbornness I'd inherited from my father.

Yet the curse of my birth would not fully disappear. How could it when everyone latched onto ridiculous superstitions and continued to talk of the nix? If I wanted Nari, I would get no help in doing so. I must make a life of my own. Break free from the curse. Show everyone the tale of the nix lived only in their minds.

And now, the time was nigh. I stood on the precipice of my future, where panic fought with logic, and I wasn't sure which would win.

We sat in our tree, legs dangling freely on either side of the branch. I pulled Nari's back against me and wrapped my arms around her. As we huddled together, she glanced up at me. "If you look this filthy, I am afraid of what I look like." She took out an embroidered square and twisted to rub at my cheek.

I admit, I wasn't really listening. I chose to follow the twists and dips of my mind, and at every bend, I found no peace, for the answers to my dilemma were not easily gained.

Slowly, she stopped what she was doing and lowered the cloth. Cocking her head to the side, she nudged my ribs. "What are you thinking?"

Startled out of my thoughts, I stared out over the treetops, concocting a quick lie. "Well. If you need to know—"

"Truth, Ryne."

"What?" I slanted a quick look at her.

She pushed out of my arms. "I can always tell when you're thinking up a lie to protect me."

She could? "How?"

"Never will I tell. So come clean. Where is your mind?"

In turmoil. In Hades. I slumped forward as defeat rushed through me. "I wish I could bring your father something special, something to show him I would make a good son-in-law."

Although my father often told me I had more talent than any man he'd ever met—certainly my wife would not starve, but neither would she find abundant wealth—I'd always been taught that a man can never know too much. Success depended upon diversity. I could lay stone, till the soil, and hunt. All good professions in themselves, to be sure, but with my doomed future riding my shoulder, a woman's father would have to be very sure he did not give his daughter's hand away in vain.

"You still think of Tait, don't you? He's an idiot. Conceited and without worth."

"My thoughts are far more disturbing than he." And they shook me to my core.

She waited patiently for me to continue, but I feared her answer.

A gentle hand came to rest on my thigh. "You can trust me, Ryne."

My gaze softened when I looked at her. "Very well. Can you tell me, is your father superstitious?"

She sighed and lifted her hand to pick at the tree bark. "No more than anyone else."

"There are a great many superstitious people living around here."

"You are thinking of the nix."

I threw her a quick glance. "I'm surprised you dare speak of it."

"I would dare much for you. Even a curse."

I looked away. The nix was a sore subject between us. The new wife had made her views known when it came to my family and their odd connection to our village history. Though Nari professed the whole thing a hurtful fancy that only led to gossip and hate, the new wife thrived on keeping the tale uppermost in people's minds. Who wanted a poor son-in-law, and one doomed to die?

"How can I not think of the tale?"

"My father is as practical a man as the nix is fantasy. You have nothing to worry about." She flipped my shirt collar and wrinkled her nose. "Except that he will turn you away for the dirt clinging to your shirt."

"Why disparage the good Lord's earth? It proves I am unafraid of hard labor."

A teasing glint entered her eyes. "Or that you are so afraid of the nix you refuse to take a bath." With that, she scampered down the tree and stood looking up at me arms akimbo. "Come. Be the man I know you are. Take me as your wife or leave me be. The choice is yours."

She was so utterly gorgeous standing there in her dirty linens. "You are a cruel woman to offer me so tempting an escape."

"You will not have me, then?"

I leapt from the tree and landed next to her. Standing tall, I took her hand and kissed it tenderly, gazing over our hands and into her sparkling blue eyes. "You cannot be rid of me so easily."

"Good." She tucked the small square into my hand and her mouth quirked up at the edges. "A token of my love. Now off with you. I'll see you tonight. Clean and pretty."

"I cannot wait."

I watched her saunter down the lane, her hair bouncing saucily and her hips wiggling provocatively. And for the thousandth time I sighed. No luckier man lived than me.

The day was growing short. I'd taken a bath and now made haste through the house, avoiding my father's stare and my mother's sudden fit of gentle weeping. God's truth, I'd expected surprise, but tears and wary looks all because I'd confessed my love for Nari and our wish to wed?

My father stood by the fire, his gaze alternating between it and me. If he expected to divine my future from the ashes, he would be disappointed. I knew better than anyone what course to take. I had confidence even if he did not.

"This is what you want? *She* is who you want?" he asked in quiet tones.

"More than I can say," I shot over my shoulder

Where had I put that shirt? I quickly rummaged through a short stack of clothes. I needed to look my best tonight; my future depended on it.

My mother sniffled lightly. "She was a wild child, ever into one trouble or another—"

"Just as I was," I jumped in, defending my love. The shirt found, I clutched at my trews barely hanging on my hips, and hiked them higher. I needed a belt. My gaze careened round the room, searching for even a piece of string to hold up the sagging cloth. Ah-ha. There the belt lay, draped over a chair in the corner. I snatched it up, nearly knocking my mother over in my haste.

Gentle hands took hold of my arm and turned me around, forcing me to stare into her watery eyes. I had avoided their probing in fear they held condemnation for my choice. Yet, no censure could I find. Only love. "But I do believe she has grown into a fine woman, and I cannot find a fault. My tears are of a mother's loss. My son is grown."

"But are they compatible?" my father asked, coming alongside my mother to drape an arm over her shoulders. His concern was no less than my mother's and he was far more vocal than she. "Do you complement each other?"

I faced him. "Does the sun complement the moon? Does the flower complement the meadow? Nari and I are suited in a way that scares me, for if I cannot have her, I may well die."

A tremulous smile touched my mother's lips and she patted my arm. Not so my father. Worry etched deep lines between his brows. "Her father may well refuse you."

"He won't. I'll make him agree." I shrugged on my shirt, threw on the belt and bounded out the door.

My parent's followed me to the threshold where the sniffles of my mother spurred me on.

"Be smart about this, Ryne," my father warned. "Tread softly, for no man willingly gives up his treasure."

I stopped in my tracks and cast a hopeful backward glance. "Is that a blessing, then?"

My father's firm face softened. "If you love her, then so shall we. Godspeed, son."

A sudden lightness infected my being, as if the heavens had opened and the stars shone down on me and only me. I gave my parents a distracted wave as I strode toward the village. Tonight, I would persuade Nari's father to let us marry.

My trip to her door was uneventful. I hesitated, and pulled her gift from my pocket, a symbol of her affection. My calloused thumb rubbed over the design. Small beads stitched securely, and bright threads locked in a pleasing manner to form a series of wild flowers surrounding her monogram. She would have to create a new one, for soon the letters would change. She would be mine.

Putting the cloth away, I stepped to the door and unlike before, this time I knocked with decided purpose. With Nari's love in my heart, I had no fear.

The door sprang open to reveal the sour expression on the new wife's face. "Again? My rock chimney fair gleams with new stone, my walls are straight and the stable will withstand the strongest gale. What more would you fix?"

"I am pleased all is well. May I inquire if your husband is home? I wish to speak with him."

She narrowed her tiny eyes. "About what?"

"It is of import between him and me."

"We are philanthropic only to the poorest of the poor."

"I wish no money." And worse, I'd none to give.

"You wish no work and you wish no money? A fine thing that. What can a lad like you wish to gain by speaking with my husband?"

"Ryne," Nari's happy voice sounded behind the new wife.

It was as if the light finally dawned. Could she really have been that ignorant of the love blossoming beneath her own roof? Even though Nari and I kept our meetings private, everyone we met seemed to cast us curious looks. Clearly, the new wife had not wanted to see what was taking shape before her. But she did now.

"Oh no you don't," she leaned forward and snarled. "I'll not have you curse this family, too. What kind of love would have a man subject a woman to such a terrible life? I'll see her off to work the piggery before you have her. And she'll thank me for it in the end, I'll wager."

She pulled back and made to close the door when a large hand interrupted her plans. Nari's father forced the door wider until his weather-roughened face peered out at me. "Ryne. What brings you here?"

"He was just leaving," the new wife insisted and shot me a glance daring me to disagree.

I would not be put off.

I swallowed hard and faced Nari's father. "I beg only a moment, sir."

"I told him we need no more of his services, but he is persistent, and not to his credit."

"Is he?" The tall man lifted his pipe and clamped the stem between his big, strong teeth.

The new wife cast me a triumphant smirk. "He is. Send him off, my love. We need not be bothered at our own door."

Puffs of smoke ringed his face while he looked me up and down. Sweat prickled the back of my neck, but I did not squirm. I held my ground and regarded him with an open countenance.

After a long moment, as the new wife continued to mutter her usual doom and gloom predictions regarding my future, he nodded. "You are just in luck. I find myself with a stack of spare moments. Come join me for a spell."

"God preserve us." The new wife threw up her hands and rolled her eyes toward heaven. "No good will come of this. No good, I tell you."

Nari rushed ahead and placed two chairs by the fire. As I stepped inside, she motioned me toward the chair she stood behind, her face wreathed in a luminous smile. I could barely breathe against my rising panic. My father's words reverberated in my head. What if he refuses?

After greetings that included news of my parents and how business faired, he stopped talking and stared straight into my soul. Nari had moved behind her father and now nodded her head at me encouragingly.

"Sir," I squeaked, and then swallowed and tried again. "Sir," I managed in a more manly tone, "I have come to ask for Nari's hand in marriage."

I was fair pleased I said it all without a single stutter.

The new wife moaned her distress which morphed into a loud keening that shook the plates and rattled the candles until they tilted in their stems. Her distress was so loud, it was sure to draw the neighbors.

"Woman," Nari's father shouted, "desist your howling. I cannot think amid the noise."

Shocked at the force of her husband's demand, for he was not one to lose his temper in all the years they had been married, the new wife abruptly sputtered to a stop, granting the quiet he requested.

Nari's father didn't so much as blink during his outburst. His gaze stayed fixed on me in a most discomforting manner.

Silence stretched, gobbling up minutes as greedily as the night catches shadows. Soon, the pre-dusk hour had sunk into evening and all that illuminated the room was a small fire and a few slanting candles.

"Tell me the tale."

"What?" I could not have heard him correctly. But I had. I could see it in his questioning eyes. "You know it. Everyone for miles does."

Nari's father cast a quick glance at the new wife. "I've heard rumors …"

My stomach tightened uncomfortably. "I can't stop people from talking."

"I suspect–can only imagine–'tis a painful condition you've been forced to endure."

"At times…" I frowned. What was he getting at?

His gaze intensified, narrowing to peer at me through the veil of pipe smoke. "And do you believe your father?"

"He…"

What could I say? I would never disgrace my father to anyone. He was a good man. The best of men. My jaw grew stiff; my tongue thick. I looked down at my hands. My knuckles had turned white as they gripped my knees painfully. "My-my father would never lie."

"It is what I believe…"

I glanced up at Nari's father. The smoke from his pipe curled lazily around his head, drawing my gaze to the taut skin around his eyes. When I wasn't looking, he had taken hold of Nari's hand, a simple enough gesture, but there seemed to be a deeper meaning to it–a protective act.

I straightened in my chair, squaring my shoulders and looking him in the eye. "I would love and honor Nari for the rest of my life."

"I know you would, but what kind of life would that be? One filled with ridicule? You can't pretend not to know. Gossip follows you everywhere. If she married you...well..."

My heart skittered roughly in my chest and my lungs ached as my breathing suddenly stilled. I saw my once full future spin back in time to the moment of my birth and my father's fantastical tale of a beautiful yet vengeful nix who lived in the lake. I'd never stood a chance at a normal life. Never.

Within the horror of the moment, a seed of anger burst forth. Yet again, I was being defined by a tale that held no truth. Everyone thought they knew me. Everyone had their own opinions about me and my family. I had tried to defy the superstition that determined my place in the village, but it hadn't mattered. I was and would always be doomed.

I quickly stood and executed a quick bow. My throat convulsed as I gazed down at my feet. I'd tried to place them in a world of reality, but no one wished to see me there. I was a living myth. Cursed by God. A danger. Unwanted.

And he was right. I could not subject Nari to that kind of life.

"Thank you for your time," I managed to say.

I headed for the door, passing the new wife and her gaping visage, outpacing Nari and her pained expression and soft pleas to stay. But I could not remain here. How did she expect me to look at her and be content knowing she could never be mine?

Flinging myself out of the house, I came up short. The neighbors, who were drawn by that horrible keening, had collected around the door and were debating on whether they should intrude on the sorrow within. I pushed through them just as the new wife burst out. Her tale of woe rose from her lips to encompass the whole village. "Safe, my friends. We are safe, though only by a hairsbreadth did we find our luck."

I lengthened my stride, focusing on the shadows of the forest. Only there would I find peace. Only there could I lick my wounded pride.

"What disaster did you escape?" I heard a woman ask.

The new wife laughed. A laugh of the nervous. A laugh of the disbelieving. "A disastrous marriage."

I plunged into the night, ignoring my name quivering on Nari's raised voice. The plaintive cry caused me to shudder. She could not want me. Not now. Not after her father made it clear how horrible our life together would be. I didn't expect her to follow. Truthfully, I believed her father would have stopped her. I should have known better. On the surface Nari was a beautiful woman, but beneath the skin, in the depths of her soul, she was and would always be the dirt encrusted lad I'd known in my youth. A fighter. A rebel. But not a redeemer. Her family would not allow her that role, and I could not blame them.

I thundered through the woods in a random pattern. I'd forgotten who was tracking me. I expected the darkness to defeat her. It didn't. The moon shone bright, almost as if to point a silvery finger at my progress. I moved faster, quieter. I climbed over fallen trees and pushed through heavy brush that scratched my skin and tore at my hair.

When I finally made it to the pool, I collapsed in a gasping heap. No one knew of this place. Nari would never find me.

What a mess. What a hopeless endeavor. I'd been warned repeatedly, but I'd hoped. I'd dared to reach beyond what was acceptable. I'd wanted what could never be. I stared at the water, thinking of the nix and hating her more than ever before. "I'm never going to be done with you, am I? Even though you don't exist, you do to everyone else, and because of that, I'll never really be free."

The water held no answers for me. It lapped quietly at the bank, its cool, dark waters tempting yet deceitful. As the moon lost its luster to a bevy of clouds, its light muted to a soft shimmer and the sound of Nari's approach shattered the isolation I'd found. I wasn't surprised, but my heart was too broken to face her.

In a moment of weakness, I almost wished the nix were real. At least then I'd have a place. A purpose. To sacrifice oneself for the entertainment of others had to be better than living with this dull, deep pain of constant ridicule.

The water stirred as the mist swirled to life and began its journey over the gentle swells toward land. I could always count on the mist to infiltrate the forest. As soon as it did, I would do the most painful thing possible, something my father could never do. I would escape. I'd leave the village for someplace new, where no one knew me or the tale of the nix.

"Hide me," I whispered to the rising mist mournfully. Pathetically.

As if by magic, the mist rushed forward and engulfed the pool and the ground where I stood.

10

Impossible

"Ryne." Nari's voice held a muffled quality to it as if she pressed a wad of cotton in front of her mouth. She pushed further into the fog. "Are you here? Please, Ryne. I know you are." A sob caught on the last word, but she continued forward. "You have to be here."

I inched around the spot where she stood, barely making out her form in the heavy mist.

She took a step forward. "Why did you leave? Why did you let them scare you away?"

I held my tongue. It was best I melt into the forest like the myth I'd become. Over time, she'd forget all about me.

"Don't do this," she cried, moving dangerously close to the pool. "I love you. Only you. If I don't care what anyone says, why do you?"

I hesitated. I fought back the words that sprang to my tongue. She didn't know how hard life would be.

People would always be staring. Always asking. Always laughing. The new wife was right. That wasn't any way to show someone love, by subjecting them to that kind of life.

Just as I turned my back to go, I heard a sharp gasp and a loud splash. Nari had fallen into the pool. I shouldn't have worried. She knew how to swim, but I listened for the telltale sign of her climbing free of the water.

I heard nothing. No sputter. No drip of water from drenched clothes.

"Nari?"

I moved closer to the pool, blindly feeling my way. The mist was so thick, I had to get on my hands and knees and feel my way to the edge.

"Nari?" I called louder, more forcefully. At the continued silence, my heart surged. "Nari."

If she didn't surface…

I couldn't wait. I dove into the water and clawed my way to the bottom. I'd never before given a thought to how large the pool was, but now it felt never-ending as I pushed my hands out to search for Nari like a blind man would use his cane. My lungs burned, but I refused to give up. The very next moment, I found her trapped against the rocks, as if she'd been stuffed between two boulders. How had she managed it? I took hold of her face and clamped my lips to hers and blew air into her lungs. I bolted to the surface, my mind in a fog of terror, took a deep breath and dove back down. When I returned to where I'd found her, only her dress was left floating in the current. I made a quick search of the area before bolting back to the surface. When I crested, the moon had reappeared and cut a silvery beam through the mist. The play of silver light lent an eeriness to the pool, but it was the scream that sent chills down my spine.

Fear spiked through me. "Nari." I cried, twisting this way and that as I treaded water. Where was the sound coming from? It echoed again and again, ripping into my ears and into my heart. "Nari."

A deep rush of water pushed against me, and in the next instant, I was jerked beneath the surface, hurling toward the opposite side of the pool at an incredible speed. I curled toward the hands that held me, instinctively wanting to pry myself free, but as my hands touched my captor, I immediately knew the curve of that wrist. A quick glance up showed me Nari's terrified face. I didn't have time to wonder at what was going on. Our momentum suddenly slammed us into the far bank. I tried to protect her, but I wasn't quick enough. Nari hit the solid rock, and then her head lolled to the side as her grip loosed my leg. Bubbles rushed from her mouth, and she began to sink. I grabbed her with one arm and with a powerful push, I shot us toward the surface.

I sucked in air and tenderly held Nari's head above water as I clamored toward the bank. "Wake up, Nari," I begged. "I need you to wake up." I again blew air into her mouth and was quickly rewarded with her violent fit of coughing. She suddenly stiffened in my arms and began to fight me.

"It's me. Ryne," I shouted, and gave her a quick shake.

When she finally managed to recognize me, she burst into tears. When we reached the bank, I barely had to help her as she launched herself toward dry land. When she made it to her feet, she whirled around and shouted, "Hurry, Ryne. Get out of the water."

Exhausted, I pulled myself free and knelt on the bank, my head drooping between my shoulders, too tired to move another inch.

Nari knelt before me in her thin, sodden shift and stiff corset. She soon began to shiver from cold and shock. Water streaked her face and her hair stuck wetly to her neck and shoulders. She raised her quaking arms and wrapped them around my neck, molding herself to my body. I held her close, still fearing she would go limp, and sickened by the thought of her near drowning. "It's all right," I cooed soothingly. "You're safe now."

"Don't ever leave me again."

I kissed her neck, her hair and the small shell of her ear and whispered fervently, "Never. I love you, and I always will."

She hugged me tighter, whispering over and over again how much she loved me.

I rubbed her back, heating her skin with the friction of my hands and after a while, I nudged her gently away. The look in her eyes held a wildness that unsettled me and I immediately wanted to pull her close again, but I had to know. "What happened?"

"Dear God, Ryne." The shock of her voice matched that of her face. "She's real."

"Who is real?"

Her full lips thinned with alarm. "Your father was right. The tale is true."

I shook my head. "No. Listen to what are you saying." There had to be another explanation.

She took my head in her hands and forced me to look at her. "The nix is real."

The truth in her deep blue gaze scared me more than I was willing to admit.

Yet, when I opened my mouth to deny what she claimed, a pair of arms shot out from behind me and snatched me back into the pool.

The water rushed over me as Nari fell to the bank, screaming. Her arms stretched out toward where I had disappeared, her face wreathed in horror as I was pulled deeper into the water and out of sight.

Part Two

The Nix

Behold, the nix.

A creature far more comely than man,

Yet far more tragic.

11

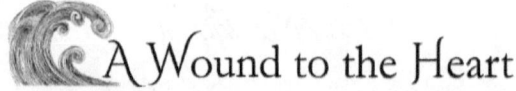A Wound to the Heart

I am the nix. I have been since the beginning, placed here by an unseen hand to tend to this lake and protect it from harm. I take what I need, surviving off the generous portions given into my care. For many, many years, in which time did not matter, the lake flourished, and I was happy living in my crystal clear, underwater playground. Not once did I wish for what I could not have. The decree that I stay in the lake and never leave was not a hardship, for I loved my world.

Then man came.

The unseen hand placed him on my shore, and I grew curious. Hiding in the thick forests of cattails and yellow iris, amid a thin wisp of mist, I watched. The man was told to tend to the earth. Day after day he toiled, back bent under the strain as sweat glistened on his skin—skin that barely changed colors. His was either pale peach in the cool morning or bright pink in the hot sun. He didn't have the array of brilliant hues I had to choose from. Even so, there was something appealing about him. Pity washed over me like the tug of the tide. It pulled ever stronger at my heart. He worked so hard for the little he harvested. Surely there was something I could do?

One day, when the man drew near the water to cleanse his hands, I acted on impulse. With a flick of my body, I gathered a small school of fish and drove them toward shore. As the wave grew, the man stood and backed away. Just when the man was about to turn and run, the wave crashed, and to his delight, fish flew from the lake and landed far ashore, flopping and flipping as they gasped in vain at the receding waters. The loss of life was great, but my love for the man had grown greater.

Far offshore, I poked my head from the water, eager to see if the man would accept my gift. Long moments passed as he surveyed the dying fish. He appeared confused, even disturbed by the unsolicited gift. Had I thought wrong? Did man not eat what nourished me? My fears were soon laid to rest as he quickly scooped up the fish and built a fire. What he did not eat, he smoked and packed away for a future meal.

The man grew healthy and strong under my care. I continued to sacrifice the fish whenever I saw him gaze longingly into the lake. But my gift was not enough. I wished to touch this man. To speak with him as others did. Yet bound by water, I could do nothing. Then one day as the mist hung close, I lingered near the shore and hid amid the tree roots, watching him, longing for him...

He saw me. It was the briefest glimpse, but that was all it took. In a panic, I dove beneath the water.

As if in a dream, he came after me, flailing against the crests, shouting for me to come back. I glanced over my shoulder. Should I? It was my heart's desire, but was it wise? I had watched him for so long...tended to his needs with a lover's care. Could he feel the same for me?

I turned toward shore. He had made it beyond the shallows. I giggled as I watched his graceless swim. Did he think to find me up there? As if reading my mind, he sank beneath the waves, and down toward me, his limbs still batting erratically at the water. I waited, circling below him. In my excitement, my skin flashed from blue to yellow to a burnt red. It had begun the change to purple when he reached me. I circled around to face him, a smile of welcome on my face and came up short. He did not look as I expected. His cheeks were ruby red and puffed; his eyes bulging. As soon as he saw me, air rushed from his mouth in a gurgle of panic, and his thrashing grew even more volatile.

He could not breathe. He would die. I immediately clasped my arms around his chest and pulled him to the surface. It wasn't enough. He had grown limp. A being of the land, he could not stay in the water. I had to get him to shore, yet I could not leave the water. A thought grew and crystallized. Closing my eyes, I called forth a heavy mist—so heavy that it shrouded the woods.

With the moisture rising thickly from the lake, I carried him to shore and laid him on his side in the gentle surge of water and foam, careful to keep my own feet planted firmly in the lake.

Water bubbled from his mouth as he sought air. With a twist of his body, he spat, and when he had expelled all the water from his lungs, he turned toward me. Unsure and with a hint of disbelief, he stared, his eyes a clear blue, like the edges of my lake on a new spring day.

I had matched my skin tone to his—a beautiful dusty

rose. Regretfully, I had no control over my hair. It dried quickly in the air, and with a self-conscious nudge, I pushed the bulk of it behind my back where it tumbled past my hips like a lustrous blue black wave.

"Who are you?" he asked, his gaze roaming my form from head to toe.

Could he not guess? I smiled and dropped to my knees beside him. He startled as I touched his skin along his jaw. "Warm," I murmured, "like the water near the surface." My fingers swept up his temple to his hair. "Soft, like the fins of angelfish."

As I continued to touch his neck and then his clothes, exploring as much of him as I dared, his skin turned a mottle pink and blue, and he began to shiver.

So his skin could change to more than two colors. I again matched my skin tone to his...though not as beautiful as the rosy hue. I only wanted to please him. When my fingers traced back up to his temple, I noticed how dry my skin had become. The mist was not heavy enough. I had to return to the lake. But not before I satisfied my longing.

I bent forward, hovering a hairsbreadth from him, drinking in every detail of his face before I bestowed on him a kiss. He immediately stopped shivering. When I pulled away, my blood sang a song of longing to him, and his lips clung to mine.

"No. Don't go," he breathed sweetly.

His skin was again the dusty rose I admired so much. I smiled and backed away.

"Will you come again? Say you will. You must."

I nodded. And with that silent promise, I slipped into the waves, and swam back to my home, rapture making my bones join my new song.

I came to him in the mist, again and again. I found

it was much easier to conjure it at night when the sun did not fight my magic. We rarely talked, but when we did, he seemed perplexed, even irritated.

His hands tightened on my shoulders. "Let me come to you tomorrow. Let me meet your family."

"You cannot."

My denial wasn't meant to be cruel, though it seemed to hurt him. I touched his face. "I have no family."

His countenance lifted. "Then you must live with me."

I shook my head.

His smile faltered. He took in my form, and then my feet which I kept firmly planted in the surf. He frowned. Hesitated. His hands shook ever-so-slightly before he peered intently into my eyes. "If you won't come with me, at least let me show you where I live. It lies just beyond the woods in a tiny glen…"

He made to draw me forward and out of the water, but I slipped back, breaking free. "I cannot."

The water was my life. If I stepped free, I would die.

As I backed away, he followed me, wading into the lake as doubt clouded his eyes. "I don't understand. I can't go with you and you can't come with me. Why?"

I placed my finger against his lips, their silky softness entranced me. I was content to kiss and love the night away. Why was not he? I found that whenever questions came to his lips, it was easier to replace them with kisses. I drew closer until my mouth met his. A song rose from my body that promised his heart's desire. I wove the magic tune about him until he clutched me to him; his arms wrapped tightly within my silky hair that he admired so much. No more questions for this night, only declarations of love and the promise of a life together. Forever.

I felt as he did. Being near him compared to no other moment. The loneliness that had existed before, which I never understood, vanished. A fervent hope that our time would never end surrounded my heart.

Then the unimaginable happened. I began to change.

My belly swelled. Embarrassed, I stayed far out in the lake, out of his sight, but he not out of mine. As the seasons changed, I listened to my love's mournful cries. His face grew streaked with tears, a phenomenon as disturbing to witness as it was fascinating. Yet, no matter how desperately he called, I would not come to him. He threatened to swim to me, but even those threats faded with time to be replaced by cold silence. No longer did he look longingly out at the water. A hardness had settled over his features that made me shiver. Winter came in vengeful flurries, and eventually he stopped coming to the edge of the lake, and I stopped visiting the surface. If I were to pass from this life, I did not want him to suffer my anguish. It was best I suffer alone.

The months of my forced solitude grew. Summer had grown ripe and the waters warm when the day came that I thought I would die. I swam into an underwater cavern set deep into the rocks and emerged from the pool of water. The cavern, with its slick walls and wet floors, was the only place where I could stand on my feet in my underwater world. A tall, overhead shaft let in a dim sliver of moonlight, revealing the two halves of the cavern. One side housed a small area just big enough to lie on, while the other side had a larger bit of land where I could sit or pace or do whatever my mood warranted. It was also where I kept my treasure—baubles and bangles and all manner of things that pleased my eye. As I made my way to the smaller shelf, the ray of moonlight caused the mica in the walls to sparkle.

The night had grown thick, and the rocks glittered like tiny stars as I crawled onto the worn rock shelf. The area gently slanted away from the water, its shape deep and long enough to cradle my body. I wrapped my arms around my distended stomach and curled my knees to my chest. I was ready to die. I had lived and loved and protected the lake. My only regret was leaving the lake unguarded. I refused to think of the man. It hurt too much.

As the pains grew, one thought comforted me. I could find no more beautiful place to take my last breath than in this small glittering world.

Instead of death, a miracle happened. A small being emerged from my body. Intense flashes of color swept her pearlized skin, but her bronze-colored hair stayed the same. I had never thought to see something so small that looked like me. Eternal love grew between us with every breath she took, and every sigh I breathed.

I stayed on the rocks for three days, suffering the pains of the air for my newborn daughter. On the fourth day, I knew it was time to take her into the water.

I slipped into the pool, my skin drinking in its nutrients. Turning, I eased my daughter into the water and held her tightly to my side. Her squeal of delight rang within the cavern, and I laughed along with her. We bobbed beneath the surface and quickly out again. Her skin plumped and her energy tripled. Her arms and legs moved as if she would swim away and explore the lake on her own. Visions of us swimming together as I showed her our world caused my heart to take flight. My daughter was a child of the lake, just like me. Without a second thought, I plunged us into the dark waters of the cavern. My pupils dilated, glowing brightly to illuminate the dark waters. I began to make our way out of the cavern when I glanced at her. A sense of alarm pinched at my nerves. My baby began to gurgle, just like her father had all those months ago. Horror struck. She needed air. I raced back into the cavern, and when I crested, her loud crying echoed against the rocks.

As the moon poured down its silvery light and cast sparkling reflections on my baby's skin, I realized she was not like me.

She was like her father.

The next few months became a daily test for her survival. I found that though she loved the water, her skin would pucker if she stayed in the lake for more than three days. Yet, if she stayed out of the lake for more than a week, her skin would crack and peel, and I had little doubt she would eventually wither into dust. As my daughter grew, the cavern no longer became a haven. Although she longed to swim, she was unable to do so without my help, and leaving a curious child on a thin ledge became problematic. It was only a matter of time before she fell in and drowned when I was forced to leave her to hunt for food.

It was then I learned to capture air. I formed a bubble for her and we explored as much of the lake as we dared. Yet in the back of my mind, I knew something wasn't right. She needed more than a rocky ledge to call home.

My decision made, I gathered a large bubble of air and we headed for the surface. Her first sight of the sun, of birds and clouds and the expanse of forest was almost as exciting as her first taste of water. It was my first taste of doubt. If the lake gave her life, the sun gave her power.

Her strength increased, her eyes sparkled. I knew if we returned to the cavern, she would wilt away. How could I ever care for this child?

One truth formed in my mind. I would suffer anything for her. Determined to solve our dilemma, I found a sheltered cove connected to a small, but deep pool of water which was fed by a gurgling waterfall. A tiny split in the rocks allowed passage between the pool to the lake and was big enough for me to slither through sideways. Water and land so close together and protected...it felt like heaven. I created a patch of thick mist so that I could stay nearby while my daughter was on shore. But I could not sustain the mist for more than a few hours into the morning. The strong summer sun eventually ripped through the trees and rubbed at my magic and caused a deep exhaustion to wash over me. I was forced to dive and circle the pool and cove, popping my head out to make sure my child was still where I had laid her before I dove again. But the agony of being apart weighed heavily on me, and I ended up swelling the mists and huddling in the shallows, slowly turning into a thin, weak shell of my former self.

The solution to my problem was hard won, but clear.

After months of torture, the days of bright sunlight were ending. Time had ripened to the moment I feared, but a moment I must face. The sharp scent of autumn, of wood smoke and rotting leaves filled the air. I slipped a necklace I'd made out of the precious stones I'd found in my pile of treasure around my daughter's neck.

She squealed and mouthed the polished, colorful rocks. I smiled. "So you won't forget where you were born," I said.

We left our shelter and swam to a section of the

lakeshore that was very familiar to me. I called upon the mist, heavier and thicker than ever before, and waded close to shore. I had never dared to go inland, and as I watched the water swirl about my ankles, my heart pounded harder and a sense of panic rose. I knew I could never leave the lake. To break from my source of life would be to die.

As I stood staring at the line between land and water, my daughter's chubby legs kicked against my hip where I held her. She was keen to explore this new place. I was not. I held her out in front of me, our faces only inches apart. "Do not stray far. When I call, you must come back." Slowly, I deposited her on the dry earth. She crawled among the debris along the shore, mouthing rocks and shells and pulling up clumps of grass by the fistful. After awhile, I faced the water and gazed out over its ever-changing face. With a heavy heart, I called out to the man. "I am here. Come to the lake."

Over a week, I stranded myself in the gentle surf, and every day I grew weaker and weaker, yet not once did the mist fail. It clung close to the lake's surface and lapped at the shore. Every now and again, I would call out in my singsong voice, enticing the man to come to the waters' edge.

My daughter crawled hither and fro, but never too far from me. And always, when night fell, she crawled to my waiting arms and curled against my chest and fell asleep. I did not close my eyes. I stared at the rippling mist, hoping desperately the man would come. I was so tired. So weak.

He would come. He must.

On the fourth night, winter's harsh breath blew against the temperate autumn days, causing a heavy frost to cover the ground. I tucked my hair around my daughter, and focused the remnants of my energy on keeping her warm even as my body grew silvery white from the crystalline accumulation.

On the eighth night, the sound of the frozen grass snapping as it was crushed underfoot warned me of his approach.

Sudden silence.

I felt his uncertainty.

"I am here," I whispered, too exhausted to move. I managed to sliver a section of the mist, making a tunnel to where I stood. I turned my head just enough to see him.

He hesitated when he saw me. Dark circles cupped his eyes. His skin held a sallow hue while his hair hung limp against his shoulders. The months we had been apart had not been kind to either of us.

Two bright splotches flared against his cheeks. "You come now? After all this time?" His breath sounded harsh and cold, completely unlike the sleek tones I'd grown to love.

My blood had grown thick from the cold and my movements sluggish. "I had no choice," I said, gathering my arms closer to support the cradle they made. I slowly turned and showed him the sleeping baby within the crook.

He stopped his approach and stared at our child. I brushed my hair from her face. "Do you know what this is?"

"Where did you find her?"

"She is our child. I need your help. She cannot live in the lake. To survive, she needs to walk on land."

Our daughter sighed in her sleep. Her fist clutched at the necklace and her lips tipped into a soft moue. An involuntary flash of her favorite color, a light, creamy orange, swept her small body. The smallest gift from her gave me pure pleasure. Smiling, I struggled to match my skin tone to hers.

"No," the man shouted and stumbled back, pulling a knife from his belt and waved it threateningly. "What evil is this? Away with you. Away."

I frowned, confused as he staggered left and right, searching for a break in the mist. I took a stiff step forward. "Please, don't go. If you loved me at all, you will not go."

He grew still and turned wild eyes on me. His skin had turned as pale as the moon. I waded further ashore until only the bottoms of my feet felt the pull of the lake. Without my full attention, the mist had weakened drastically and my skin cracked and bled. I kissed my daughter's brow and placed her at his feet. The strain of creating the mist while keeping her warm finally grew too much; the mist fell away and I collapsed into the water. With the last of my strength, I called forth a powerful surge that enveloped my body and pulled me toward the deeper water.

Just before I let the healing waters overtake me, I saw him glance down at our daughter. Disgust twisted his face. A moment of unease struck me. I held out my hand toward my child, willing myself back to shore, but the lake would not do as I willed. It yanked me beneath the wintry caps.

As the surge pulled me further away, I saw the waves near shore turn a deep red. The crimson tendrils spread wickedly. My mouth opened on a silent scream. A splash disturbed the stain, and when the water settled, my baby's pale body floated lifelessly above me. My body contracted with horror. I sank further into the depths of the lake where a chill settled in my bones, and as my heart ripped in two, darkness closed in on me.

Never would I be the same. Never.

The man had taught me the meaning of love. Now he taught me how to hate. In the days that followed, he called others to the shore, his voice a frantic cry in the icy air. "A devil creature lives in the lake, an unnatural thing to behold. It takes the form of a beautiful woman. But be warned. She enchants. She deceives. She will rip our souls from us."

The look of madness on his face revealed the truth to the villagers. He had encountered the creature. His soul had gone. The others muttered their alarm, and he grasped onto the chokehold of fear. "We must catch her," he cried. "Haul her ashore and kill her.

Panic rippled through the crowd. They built boats and fashioned netting. They skimmed over the water, their faces peering into the depths waiting to spear me like an ill-fated fish.

No one crosses me. I gladly called down vengeance on all who dared enter its waters. With wind, rain and large swells, I capsized boats. I sang sweetly to some, while for others I placed gold coins near the shallows as an enticement into my trap. I exploited their fears, calling forth the scaly beast that lived in the depths or encouraged their deepest desires as I slithered toward them. I took and I took, fathers and sons, the confident and the bold, always hoping this time it was him, this time I would finally find peace, daring my lover to end the killings by showing his face above the waters. But he never left the shore, and my pain never wavered, and the years grew until even the bravest refused to come and find me. Hate, deep and raw, infused my bones. All men were wicked and worthless.

The legend of the lake took firm root. I heard

whispers from shore, fearful, terrified whispers. "Death will come to any who dare enter those waters."

The years grew silent. My heart turned to stone. All had listened and believed.

All except one.

12

At Last

Man's time is not mine. He is a moment on the earth while I have always been. When the waters were mine alone, and I was secure that no man would ever hunt in them again, I abandoned my vigilance of the surface. But I was not pleased. I retreated into my cavern; the ache of betrayal still stung.

I gathered the remnant bones of my daughter, and tucked them into a small niche where I could seek them out, touch them and forever speak to her. Barely surviving, barely caring what happened beyond my home, I fell deeper into hate—the hollow, bony shell of my last victim chained forever to the wall as a souvenir of my fury. So wrapped up in my misery, I did not notice when a fisherman dared to collect the bounties of my lake. He fished at will and learned his craft well. When the slap of the net and the cry of the fish finally found me, I was enraged. Who would dare such a feat after all this time?

Did he believe the curse would not find him? I

vowed to do to him what I'd done so many times before. I never expected to get caught in his nets. In my weakened state, I could not fight my way free. When our eyes met, I saw a man much like the man I'd known all those years ago—a handsome man, strong and confident. I hated him on sight. When I gained my freedom, I attacked. Yet my lure of song did not work on this man. I knew he was tempted. How could he resist my call? An impasse settled over us.

I listened to the flow of his mind and found there the impending birth of his child. His only regret was that he might never see his family again.

My gaze sharpened on the fisherman. I had found my own net and I would entwine it around this man, choking the life from him, for if I could not destroy the father now, I would destroy him through his child. I offered up a bargain so clever, he would agree.

He did…and he repaid me with deceit.

Man had not changed. He was as evil and cunning as ever.

How had I failed to lure this man? I tumbled the question in my head for many years, and only one answer remained. Magic. I felt it that day. It rolled off the man, searing my mind and weakening my strength.

But I had magic of my own. Deep magic. Dark magic. And time rested on my side. I would collect on our bargain and finish the deed I started long ago. I had no choice. We had set a price for his freedom, and I could not rest until it was paid. So, I watched. Waited. And I grew stronger with each passing day.

In the beginning, I trolled the shore, weaving in and out through the thickly bladed reeds as I waited for the babe, but my vigil came to naught. They withheld him from me.

I was not dissuaded. I had developed longstanding patience. As the babe grew into a boy, I let the wind carry a magical message only he could hear. "Find the pool."

Early in the mornings, as the mist rolled along the surface of the lake, I called to him, and he followed, with bow and arrow, he dove into the forest surrounding the lake. It was only a matter of time before he found the pool. When he did, he cast it longing glances, but still never dared the waters. My frustration grew, and I retreated to the depths. I languished there in a black mood, causing the rift in my soul to widen beyond repair.

But then the boy turned into a youth–a handsome, strapping lad–and his daring took hold. He braved the waters of the pool. I knew the moment he entered, but as luck would have it, he left before I could conjure a mist. So I returned to my cavern and formulated a plan.

I went on the prowl, keeping him in my sights by using a shell and fish blood to scry on his every move. All else fell dormant as I anticipated the moment he would draw near. A few times I came close to taking him, but it was not to be. Until now.

His time was nigh. I felt it in my bones.

As the dark blood swirled within the hollow of the mollusk shell, I saw the son draw near. The conditions were ideal. The moon was high and the mist hovered over the lake awaiting my command. With a confidence I hadn't felt in a very long time, I tossed the shell away and abandoned the cavern. I called the mist to shore, and as I rode the waves into the secluded cove, his lingering wish found me.

"Hide me," he rasped.

The mist suddenly swelled even faster than I had ever called forth. It was his doing. His wish that enhanced my magic. I smiled. He was ripe for the taking.

As I entered the pool, a large splash brought me up short. A woman fell in and her heavy dress pulled her straight to the bottom. Watching her sink, I remembered spying her with the boy, holding hands, talking. As she struggled to swim, a flash of her magic invaded my senses, a magic that felt familiar, yet tainted.

Then I remembered. The fisherman's magic. The same magic I'd felt for my child, and at one point her father. Without warning, my anger boiled against this woman. The thick darkness kept her from seeing me, which was to my advantage for I could see as well at night as I could in the light of day. I rushed forward and sank my nails into her shoulder. At my grasp, a wall of bubbles sprang from her lips. I pulled her to the rocky edge and forced her body between two boulders. Satisfied she could not loosen herself, I darted away. This was a fine moment. The boy would lose his love and then his own life.

Another splash rippled the surface. The boy–now a man–had enter the water. His blind, hectic movements spoke of his alarm. Could he actually be searching for the woman? Curiosity held me still. It took only a few moments before he found her. Cupping her face, he gave her his own air, and then left for the surface to capture another breath. Shock at his sacrifice held me captive for a moment. He could not breathe underwater, yet he dared his own death to offer her life?

Confusion rattled me. My chest grew strangely tight. I returned to the woman who was frantically climbing out of her dress. With a quick jerk under my hand, the dress tore and she broke free. She began her rise to the surface, but I snatched her back down. Her gaze widened behind the veil of her floating hair. Air bubbled from her mouth as a panicked look crossed her face. Movement from above cause me to glance up, and I saw the man coming back. That would not do. I darted away, dragging the woman toward the waterfall and the grotto located just behind it.

The falls thundered in my ears as I pulled the woman to the surface. She sputtered and wheezed and raked her hair from her eyes as I curiously looked on. What was it about the woman that made him willing to give up his life? Wet and half drowned, she had all the appearance of a weak human.

I was wrong.

With my attention diverted, the moon broke through the mist, casting a bright shaft of light against the waterfall and illuminating the crystalline walls of the grotto for a split second before I thickened the mist again. But a moment was all it took. She saw me. With a gasp, she lashed out, raking her nails down my skin and drawing blood. I screeched in anger, camouflaged my skin a midnight blue and leapt forward, drawing my own blood-laced revenge.

She backed herself against the rocks and blindly kicked out. Her feet rammed against my chest, which propelled me backwards. My surprise quickly turned to fury. Gathering my strength, I dove, sank my nails into her arm and yanked her under. We sped into the pool and passed the man, but she managed to latch onto him and drag him beneath the surface as well.

As I wrestled with the woman, I felt their magic combine. It grew until it fairly burned my skin. I had no choice but to release her, but I did so by slamming them into the rocks. Her head hit with a satisfying thunk.

I receded into the depths of the pool and clutched my stinging hand to my body as I glared up at them. My anger smoldered brighter than ever. They struggled together for a moment and then scrabbled for the bank where they helped each other from the pool. How dare they defile my world. How dare they use the father's magic against me.

Through my strength I'd weakened them. As I stared up through the water, I saw him collapse to his knees on the edge of the pool. He had faced his worst nightmare and survived. He must think himself invincible. It was time to show him how utterly foolish and vulnerable he really was.

13

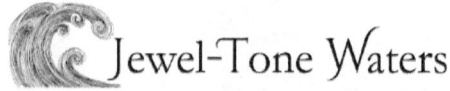
Jewel-Tone Waters

I no longer cared about the woman. With the man gone, surely she would turn away and wither into dust. It was him and only him I wanted. With wicked pleasure, I pushed off the bottom of the pool. The water sang past me as I launched myself from the water. Droplets fanned out around my body, their weight holding me aloft for a moment before I wrapped my arms around his torso and pulled him into the depths of the pool.

This time, I did not waste one moment. I snatched the clothing along his nape and pulled his struggling form behind me as I slithered through the gap that separated the pool from the lake. He clawed at the rocks, securing a handhold, but I would not be denied. After a kick to his head and a sharp tug, he let go, and I headed straight for deeper water, past the cattails and thick reeds that choked the banks of the lake, skimming over submerged boulders tufted with algae, and between long submerged tree roots that formed hollowed shelters for fish. The deeper we dove, the colder the water became, and its color turned from pale green to turquoise blue to dark sapphire.

Long ago, I'd taken a man to the very depths of the lake and watched as the air inside him grew smaller and smaller and then not at all. When I let him go, his frantic churning toward the glittering surface had disturbed the beast. The man's last moment of life showed him the manner of his death. Whether he drowned or died of fright, I did not know and I did not care.

Of all the men who dared the lake, the fisherman's son deserved a special death. I'd been deceived by the father and led on a merry chase by the son, yet I no longer cared how he died. I was physically tired, and weary of the pain that ripped into my soul. I wanted him gone from this world, now and forever.

The weight of dragging him suddenly lightened. I turned to see he had slipped out of his shirt. I cared not. I let the shirt go. We had gone farther than I knew he could swim for air. It was time to watch him take the last breath of his life. He tried to move his limbs, but they refused to obey. His dark hair floated around his handsome face and his skin had turned translucent, showing the bluish-green veins lying just beneath his skin. A spasm rippled through his body as he fought the urge to flood his lungs with water. The struggle was useless. He had no choice.

"Do it," I commanded, impatient for his death. "End this now."

He grasped my shoulders, his fingers burning into my skin as he pulled me close. Too close. I could see my reflection in his gaze, the current's wild whipping of my hair as it framed the malevolence of my face. His eyes suddenly rolled back in his head, freeing me of the disturbing image, and air gushed from his lungs. He took a deep gulp. The muscles in his neck bulged in his last moments of panic.

I smiled as I witnessed his soul being banished from his body.

It took a pain-filled moment until he went completely limp. His fingers loosened. His hands slowly drifted away from me.

It was done. The bargain met. The price paid.

The lake gently tugged at his body, pulling it further away. But the tightness in my chest still hurt. Images of his devotion to the woman haunted my mind…and one question kept surfacing. Why?

Man had once shown me preference. He had lavished on me his attention and swore his everlasting love. But it had been a false promise. I realized now it was love that had burned me when I sought to harm the woman—their love for each other. It was stronger than me, more wild, more secret than I could know. It had fought for her life and won.

But it hadn't been enough. He was dead. Now I would find the peace that evaded me. Yet, as I watched the lake claim his body, I felt no peace. My heart became a dead weight within my chest, scarred anew by the life I was forced to endure.

As he floated further away, his body jerked. Once. Twice.

His eyes shot open and his shocked sky-blue gaze looked straight at me.

My heart leapt to life. Once again, I'd been betrayed. He had not drowned. He was as surprised by the notion as I, and that leaned toward my favor. I rushed at him, wrapped my fingers around his throat and squeezed.

He must die. He. Must. Die.

Pain seared through my fingers and into my palms. I yanked them away, howling my offense. I gaped stupefied at the red hue of my hands and the throb of burned flesh. My gaze whipped back at him. His throat was as lily white as always. Not a mark to be found. I rushed him again, baring my teeth at his neck, but as soon as they touched his skin, a jolt of pain flashed through my body, shocking my senses and tumbling me away.

I shook off the shock and stared horrified at the man. What manner of magic infused this being?

Anger tore at my soul and again, I attacked him, only this time I latched onto his thick, dark hair and towed him deeper into the lake.

Schools of fish, their silver bodies flashing their alarm, darted out of my way as I took him to my long-ago haven, the only land my feet could touch. Our heads broke through the calm waters of the cavern, and with little care, I threw him onto the cold rocks. He landed hard, scraping his skin raw, but he rolled to the side and back onto his feet, spitting water from his lungs. Though his body had grown even paler and he had begun to shiver, he crouched low as if he were prepared to fight.

His eyes glittered sharply. "W-what kind of magic did you w-wield to allow me to breathe underwater?"

I cocked my head and narrowed my eyes, the sting of my hands still present and painful. How dare he play me false. "None of mine, human, as you well know."

His legs shook and he collapsed to his hands and knees, though his voice rose in a hoarse, threatening snarl. "You can't keep me here."

"Maybe not. But I will try." With that, I dove and exited the cavern. I hovered by the entrance and called into the deepest part of the lake. The waters reverberated with an answer, and I waited.

I could feel the human behind me, waiting for a chance to slip by. As he crept closer and closer to the entrance, a warm, stiff current heralded the creature's approach. Out of the darkness, a triangular head—its width wider than the nearest boulder—slithered into view. A pair of boney fins flanked each side of its head, as if they were large ears beating the water for sound. Yellow eyes, set deep in its head, glowed as they scanned the area, and a pair of sharp horns sat atop the skull like two spokes of a crown. Its long neck came into view, followed by a sleek, scaly form, and the wings—perfect for swimming or flying—lashed out from its body as the ancient creature moved lazily forward. Its claws churning up the bottom until it came to rest beside me. The vivid purple of its scales melded into a cool green and then pale white, enabling it to hide in the deepest depths or far up in the air. It was a magnificent creature so ancient and so hated by man, it had been hunted into near extinction.

There existed an affinity between the beast and I, an awareness that we were the last of our kind. I placed a tender-palmed hand on the sharp angles of its head. "You know the ills which have befallen me. You know the evil that is man."

The creature stared its understanding, and I moved aside so it could see into the tunnel leading to the cavern and to the human hovering nearby. The man's face paled. Shocked disbelief warred with his desire to leave, but even he knew the likely results of his escape. Slowly he faded back toward the cavern and out of view. I stroked the large head. "If he comes out, eat him."

The human would not be so reckless as to wander out now. As the dragon settled, I made my way to the surface. Pushing through the reeds and weeding through the roots of the lily pads, I scoured the banks for the woman. She held the key to my woes and to the magic that kept the man alive. I knew that truth as deeply as I knew every rock and creature that inhabited my lake. But I saw nothing of her. No human at all. For two days and two nights I waited, and by the third morning's light, I returned to the cavern, and to the man who would not die.

14

Scrying

I entered the cavern and eased my head above water, staying quiet as I gazed at the man who had caused me so much trouble. The last I'd seen of him, he had been huddled against the rocks, scared but defiant. I thought he would find no such comfort here, but I was wrong. He now lay in a circlet of sunlight, gathering as much warmth as his pathetically mottled pink and blue skin could catch and hold before the spot disappeared. Though his pants had finally dried, they lay against his body ripped and tattered from the violence of our meeting, and were hardly thick enough to give him protection in this damp environment.

He reached out and picked through my treasure, selecting a large stone.

"See, my friend," he said to the skin and bones chained to the far wall. "We are surrounded by riches. Fat lot it does you or I, pretty though it all may be."

He blew the dust free and held the stone up for

inspection. The glow of azure fire colored his fingertips, shooting rays of blue around the cavern and lighting his face a soft cerulean.

Handsome still. Even in this moist and dark place, he could woo a woman to give her heart away. And that was my problem. The woman's love for him kept him strong. Somehow, I had to break that bond. Weaken him by weakening her.

He pulled out a small square of cloth and handled it lovingly. A whisper filled with longing sounded. "For you, Nari." He wrapped the stone within, and brought it to his lips for a kiss. "Have faith, my love. I will come back."

A sudden rise of anger captured my heart. My skin flicked from orange to red to purple and then back again. "You dare steal?" I snarled.

His head jerked toward me, and with lightening speed, I bolted straight up, snatched the cloth from his fingers, and slid back into the water before he could even blink an eye.

He shot to his feet and warily watched me as I darted to the opposite shelf. I flung the fish I'd caught and the cloth wrapped rock next to each other before pulling myself free of the water.

"I have no complaint with you." he said. "I have done nothing to warrant your attack."

He would appeal to my mercy? He'd soon find out I had none. "Your kind has done more harm against me than you know. I am within my rights. This is *my* lake. *My* home. All have been warned away. But your father chose not to listen. And when caught, like a coward, he panicked. He deserves to die. Your complaint is with him, for he set the price which you must now pay."

I took up the fish and ripped it open from gill to tail over the mollusk shell. Blood gushed from the wound along with the slick mound of its innards. I picked the unwanted bits from the shell and swirled the blood, blowing on its surface. "Show me the woman," I rasped, blowing and asking…blowing and asking again and again. "Show me."

The man leaned forward, his interest keen on what I did on the far side of the cavern. I ignored him. The blood bubbled and then grew still. I tucked my feet beneath me and peered deeply, waiting for the visions to appear.

The image of the woman grew clearer, taking form to reveal her kneeling by the lake, crying. I cast my gaze on the man. "Your woman thinks you're dead. She cries for you."

"What?" He staggered forward, coming close to the edge that would see him in the water again. "You see her?"

"I see and hear many things. She has not eaten since you left. Soon she will be no more." If only it were that easy, but I knew better. There was a power the pair possessed that I could not fight.

I watched his face cloud with misery. Good. Let his heart ache. Let it be drained of all hope. Let him share my pain of love found and then lost. I peered into the shell. Desperation caused my hands to clutch the shell tightly. "Tell me what to do. Tell me how to break their bond."

"What did you say?" he barked across the expanse.

I blocked out his voice and concentrated on the blood's glassy surface. A thin whisper of magic trailed through my head.

When the woman of man
believes his love for her is no more,
victory will be yours.

"But to say he is alive," I muttered to myself as a

frown burrowed against my brow, "will that not give her hope?" It could, but I had no other choice. The bond must be broken.

A rock skittered across the ground in front of me. I slanted a heated glare at the man.

"Nari has nothing to do with this." His voice grew more desperate. "I'm the one you want. You've won."

Ignoring him, I set aside the bowl and grabbed the cloth. It should not be too difficult to convince the woman of his fickle heart. I touched a bundle of cloth set in a niche, a reminder that man was not to be trusted.

"What do you plan? Tell me." His roar echoed against the confining rock walls.

My gaze snapped back to him. He paced the shelf, his face as fierce as a dragon's snarl. Wild eyed, he raked his hand through his hair, then stopped and faced me. His color deepened while I rose mutely to my feet.

"Tell me," he shouted.

His overwhelming concern delighted me. A wicked smile touched my lips. "It shall all be over soon."

With that, I dove back into the water, his shouts to come back following me through the tunnel and into the lake.

Evening had come twice since I'd taken the son, and now it approached again. I called on the mist and followed the shore. The droplets grew light on my skin— the mist non-threatening to any who would see it. I wove it between the Merlin's grass and sweet rush, slithering to a stop just beyond where the woman knelt. Her hands were wrapped in her hair, her body bent double with undisguised pain, and a man stood behind her, far older than her, with a fretful face.

"Come away, my child," he said gently, reaching out to her.

When he touched her shoulder to pull her to her feet, she jerked away. "No. Don't touch me. I will never leave this place. Never."

"Don't say such things. I know your pain. I know you loved him. But he is gone."

She covered her ears and shook her head. "Stop saying that. It isn't true. He lives. I know he does."

A younger man came forward and an older woman followed. She put her hand to the younger man's arm, stopping him. "Your sister mourns. There is nothing we can do."

This was her family. I looked on with interest.

The brother shrugged off the mother and hissed, "We can't let her stay here like this. Even you aren't that heartless."

A gasp followed his words, and the mother stepped back as if she'd been stung.

"Gordie," the father warned.

The mother's watery gaze fell on the kneeling woman. "I shed tears for her, too. Who would not when faced with such heartache. *This* is why I sent him away. *This* is what I wanted to avoid. He was doomed from birth. 'Tis a sad ending to his sad life. And what are we left with? Nothing but an empty hurt, a hurt that touches us all. Oh," she lamented in a keening tone, "the talk that will find us. Because of Nari, we now share in his doom."

The brother threw a disgusted look at their mother. "Can you think of no one but yourself?"

"I-I—" The mother turned away, her hand to her trembling lips, her gaze downcast.

The father turned his back on his wife and faced his son. "As hard as it is for me to admit, she is right in that we can do naught for your sister but wait for the pain to subside."

"And when will that be?" the younger man demanded to know.

"Never," the younger woman's lifeless voice rose eerily. She hunched down further, salty tears falling into the water as she dragged her fingers through the wet sand and gentle surf.

I peeked at the scene through the reeds. Such sadness had deep power. I could feel the magic of her tears and feared they would command the waves to bring her love back. I must stop her, and soon.

"Come away, my love and rest," the mother said, pulling her husband toward her and the village that lay beyond.

He hesitated, "I have not been the father I should have been...nor you the mother she deserves."

The older woman glanced at her daughter, and then at her son who stared contemptuously back. Tears threatened to burst when she looked to her husband. "You don't know what you're saying. You are a good man." She then cast a humble, yet pleading look toward the younger man, and said in a weak voice, "Gordie will stay with her, won't you?"

In the end, he nodded and escorted the older couple out of sight. I saw my chance and pushed through the reeds to where the young woman knelt.

As the mist thickened, she suddenly grew tense. Her head snapped up and she peered out over the lake. I pushed against the wet air until she had a clear view of me as my head crested the water.

She grabbed a handful of sodden skirt and stood. Without even a flinch of concern, she waded into the lake. "Give him back," she cried heatedly.

No timid woman this. She snapped her jaws as threateningly as a dragon. With surprise, I realized I did not scare her. Even though I'd nearly drowned her, she would face me full on and risk her life.

"Nari. Where are you? Nari." The brother had returned and sounded alarmed as he blindly wandered the mist in search of the woman.

I threw up my hand toward the woman. "Stay where you are, human, or risk your own death."

With the water surging around her thighs, she stilled. Tears, again, coursed down her cheeks. "Where is he? Give him back. Please. I beg of you."

"I cannot."

"Why? He has done nothing to you."

"But he has. His fair face has stolen my heart as I have stolen his. He does not wish to return to you."

For a moment, a horrified expression shadowed her face, and then her eyes narrowed. "You lie."

She would not be easily persuaded. I colored my skin a dusty rose and waded closer. My dark hair, my greatest vanity, instantly dried and blanketed my body in luxurious waves. "Look at me. Listen to my voice. What man would wish to leave my side? None. All love me. *He* loves me. He is mine. Forever and always."

As the last word grew silent, I opened my palm. Within the center lay the cloth and the stone inside it.

On seeing the cloth, her mouth opened on a deep, shaky breath. Her arm rose and her fingers stretched out to the cloth.

"Ryne?" sounded the pitiful word.

I had her on the hook. All I needed now was to set it deep. "He bade me give this to you as proof. Take it and leave us be."

As she stared at the cloth, her tears grew dense, one after another until a constant stream flowed. They spilled into the lake and pooled around her.

The power of her tears brought forward a long-buried memory of another. He had been hurt by my abandonment. He had called out mournfully for me. I gasped amid the emotions the memory had stirred.

My hand clenched the jagged edges of the rock. My jaw grew tight.

Tears showed a human's weakness. My heart hardened against her, and I tossed the cloth-wrapped rock toward her. As it arced in the air, I dove into the waves, away from the magic that dared fight against mine. The water cooled my heated skin, and I looked back. The woman had managed to retrieve the token even as she fought the hands of the younger man who tried desperately to haul her back to dry land.

"Take her away," I sang. "He is no more."

"Where do you go? Into the lake?" the brother asked as he wrapped his arms around her and hauled her out of the water. "Do you wish to die, too? Please, Nari, you cannot do this to yourself. To us. He is gone."

"No. She was here. The nix. She was here. Ryne's alive."

Mindless wretch.

What more proof did she need? If I couldn't break through her stubbornness, my plan would be for naught. As the man fought to reason with the woman, I slipped back into the water. Agitation caused my skin to flash a brilliant display of colors, warning any creature to keep its distance.

She did not believe.

Somehow, I had to find a way to *make* her believe.

15

Death

S wimming into the cavern, the water grew murkier and murkier. Specks of dirt floated freely, and a new layer of shale and limestone that made up the cavern had settled far below. Had there been a cave-in? Had he been crushed, his bones smashed into a million pieces? The vision caused my heart to leap with joy, and I quickly surfaced. As I looked around, I noticed one thing. He wasn't there. Not one spot of mangled flesh and bone showed itself. Only a dirt-riddled mess.

Panic gripped me. I twisted back and forth, my breath coming in quick angry gasps. And then a clump of dirt splashed into the water next to me. I looked up, and there he was, hanging by his fingertips at least fifteen feet up the rock wall. His sharp intake of breath sounded as a section of the wall broke free and tumbled past his dangling legs. He quickly sought another handhold, but the limestone broke under his weight.

He fell. Hard.

A rain of dirt and debris tumbled down, and I dove

beneath the water. Rocks of varying sizes hit the pool, sinking past me, and the reverberations of stone hitting stone shook the water. When the cavern finally grew quiet, I crested, expecting no less than what I found. Rubble littered the cavern, and the man lay in a crumpled, dirty heap. Moonlight caught the glint of miniscule bits of mica that still floated in the air, and a pain wracked moan filled the cavern.

A fit of coughing followed, which meant he was bruised, but most assuredly alive. It would have been convenient if he weren't. I glanced up toward the shaft of moonlight. The opening rose more than fifty feet above us where he had tried to climb out. He was determined. Much like me.

He moaned and his eyes flutter open. Water rippled as I moved closer, drawing his attention my way. His body tensed, and his startling sky blue eyes grew large. He bit his words out in sharp staccato. "What did you do?"

"I delivered your gift."

He pushed himself to an unsure sitting position, but his gaze remained intense and focused solely on me. "You saw Nari? What did she say?"

"She cried." I delivered the news with glee.

He did not receive it as well. "What did you tell her?" he demanded, gaining his feet as his strength returned with every passing second. He was a healthy specimen. Much more than the poor soul clamped to my wall had been.

I ignored his mounting alarm, and pulled myself from the water. My hair instantly dried and fell about my hips in blue-black waves. "She will go on with her life, now. She will find another to love."

"You told her I was dead?"

"All living things die, human. Soon so shall you."

"You keep telling me that, but here I am." Shocked realization bloomed across his face. "You can't kill me, can you?"

I whirled on him. "Sudden death need not always be the goal. There are many ways to punish man. Ask him," I said, pointing to the long silent chained figure. "I can keep you here until you become mirror reflections. Or if I so will it, I can feed you bit by bit to the dragon."

He went to the man and gripped a rusted chain in his fist. "Poor devil." He cast a hateful look at me. "You are right. All living things must die."

He suddenly ripped one of the weakened chains out of the wall, the skeletal remains breaking free, and faced me. "I wonder. Does a nix bleed?"

With a swirl of his arm, the chain whipped in a wide arc, whizzing toward me and forcing me to dive back into the water. I glared up at him through the muck of his doing. How had this happened? How had he caught me off guard? Surely something was wrong with this human. He should be cowering in the corner like all the others who begged for their lives, not racing after his own death.

Anger shivered along my skin. I shoved off the bottom and flew high into the air, stretching over him as he swung the chain uselessly over his head. I landed on my feet in a crouched position and slowly straightened.

My eyes reflected the hate in his. "Your death will not be pleasant."

Holding out my hands, I called on the stones. The man swirled the chain faster, the whiz of its passing coming closer and closer. My appeal grew louder, and my fingertips began to bleed. The cavern groaned as if in pain and within a heartbeat, chunks of rock flew from their moorings, pummeling the man to his knees.

My pent up breath rushed from my lips. I was not

surprised to see he still lived. He was indestructible. I approached his beaten form, yanked the chain from his hands and snarled, "Attacking me was unwise."

He tipped his head up to reveal a multitude of abrasions. Blood oozed from dozens of cuts, yet he gave me a joyless smile and stared directly into my eyes. "Unwise mayhap, but oddly satisfying."

Fearless as ever. Just like his father.

I twisted the chain around his body and dragged him to the opposite wall, securing a new mooring for the old stake before I stood back. "Not as satisfying as me watching you starve."

"Is that how they died?" he said, nodding toward the dried up human.

"They?" I asked. I only had one trophy of my past vengeance.

"The man and the baby."

My blood went cold. My gaze went straight to the place where I'd carefully laid out my daughter's bones, but found the niche empty. I turned on him, my ire so strong, its heat dried my skin to a crackling parchment. "Where is she?"

Simpleton that he was, he only stared at me.

I flew at him, wrapped my hands around his throat and squeezed. Yet just as before, a searing pain raked at my fingers, crawled up my hand and slithered toward my elbows. I gritted my teeth, determined to hold on and finish what I'd started.

He sputtered.

The pain clawed up my arms and over my chest.

His body lurched.

My neck burned and my vision blurred. And then blackness consumed me, shutting out all sound, all sight, all touch, and I crumpled to the floor.

When I came to, I felt the cold touch of iron upon my skin. The man had wrapped the chain around my arms...and he held the slack. I moved and he jerked against the chain, causing the iron to bite into my flesh.

"So, it comes to this," he said, an exhausted, yet wicked smile on his lips. "We will both die."

"You will die. I have always been and will always be."

His smile turned knowing. "Your magic is strong, but not all powerful. Surely I will wither into a heap of skin and bones, but you..." He motioned to my flaking skin. "Without water, you will dry up into a pile of dust. A fitting end, seeing as we both win."

I dropped my gaze to see a myriad of tiny fissures running along my hands and up my arms. My anger had depleted me of moisture. I glanced at the water. A surge of fear I had not felt in a long time rushed through me. I fought against the chain and tried to wriggle loose, but he only tugged harder.

"Do you know how long a man can live without water? They say three days, maybe a week if he's very lucky." He leaned back, opened his mouth and caught several drips of water that ran down the walls and onto the floor. His gaze returned to mine, and he smiled. "I've got water. What about you?"

The cavern that had always offered protection had turned against me. It carried water that I needed to my enemy and left me dry.

I slanted a glance at the man. He lay weakly nearby, eyes closed, his strength a faint reflection of itself. I turned my back on the grinning human and wrapped my arms about my knees. Yet a smile touched my lips. I concentrated on the water. Every drop, every small bead that hung on the walls of my cave to come to me. Slowly thin rivulets began to form, colliding with others as they snaked across the floor to where I sat.

He didn't know it, but time was on my side…and I had little doubt he would die.

Part Three

Nari

Love deserves its reward.
Whether for ill or good,
It is for the beloved to decide.

16

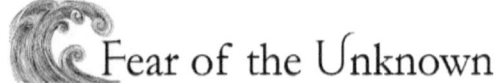

Fear of the Unknown

I lunged toward the pool, my hands grasping for Ryne–my one true love. But he disappeared into the depths, the horror of the moment etched on his face and on my brain. The mist had retreated as suddenly as it had appeared, and the moon highlighted the suddenly calm water. It was if he had never been.

This couldn't be real. My mind balked at the possibility, but my eyes did not lie.

The fear of him drowning flooded my thoughts, and I pushed it away. I would not give in; I had to save him. I dove into the pool, searching for him one blind inch at a time. Rising to the surface for air and then diving down again, the repetition put an ache in my side as the terror of not finding him climbed higher with every passing moment. On my final pass, I felt a fissure in the rocks, big enough for a man to fit through…and I knew. He was gone. The nix had finally collected her boon.

My lungs burned for air. It would be so easy to just breath deep now and end it all–the pain, the misery, the madness that had suddenly entered my life.

He is alive.

The voice whispered within my mind as clearly as if it were said in my ear.

Alive.

The crazy feeling pulled me to the surface. It made me reach for the bank and drag myself onto dry land. I gazed out over the lake. Could it be? Somewhere, out there, Ryne was alive. I knew it was true. As the mist swirled ever farther out, I curled my knees to my chest, and wrapped my arms around my legs. My body rippled with exhaustion and tears slipped down my face. My mind had frozen on one thing only. "Ryne. Come back."

What would I do without him?

I could not remember my life before Ryne. The moment I met him was the moment my life truly began. When I was younger, I adored him. When I grew older, just the sight of him sent me into clumsy fits and awkward silence. I did everything to impress him. Now, the very breath I took was done for him. He loved me. He had saved me. And what had I done?

Nothing.

Helplessness seared my mind with pain, with guilt—with longing. "Ryne."

I would not leave this spot until he returned. I would lay siege to the nix and curse her very existence. I would mourn my love until God took pity on me and brought him back.

The color of deep night gave way to pre-dawn luster when the search party, a dozen men from the village including my father, brother and Ryne's father, found me.

"Nari." My father rushed forward and sank to his knees before he wrapped me in his arms.

Shivering and delirious, I muttered Ryne's name over and over again.

I heard the men grumble, concerned for my condition, asking after my clothes and the absence of Ryne.

"What is wrong? Tell me," my father pleaded.

A crack in my litany allowed the unbelievable to be spoken. "The nix."

My father's arms tightened around me as he stared out over the lake. "That cannot be."

"What is wrong? What did she say?" the other's asked, drawing close to hear.

My father turned disbelieving eyes on them all. "The nix."

Ryne's father turned pale. "The nix came?" he whispered on a hoarse note. His handsome face, so like his son's, seemed to age ten years. The men beside him grasped his arms and supported him when his knees suddenly gave out.

My brother swung a cloak over my shoulders, and my father lifted me high against his chest. I laid my forehead against his neck and clutched at his shirt. "I cannot leave. He's alive."

My father's arms tightened, holding me closer. "No, my child. He is gone."

If I could have fought to be free, I would have, but I was too exhausted to do anything but curl against him as he carried me home.

I lay fevered for two days, and my delirium stoked their fears. The new wife's hands trembled as she bathed my brow, and my father clutched my fingers tightly when I called out my distress.

All thought Ryne was lost forever. All gave up hope.

If they thought I would do the same, they were wrong. As soon as I was able, I went back to the lake. I knelt before the waters, ignoring the tide as it lapped at my skirts, and willed the nix to appear. Tears came and went, my sadness so heavy it felt like I would never breathe again, yet I did. Each breath came as a painful reminder of the water that separated Ryne from me.

I would not eat. I could not sleep. My vigil was the only thing worth doing. My father and brother, and even the new wife, came to take me home, but I would not listen. And when the nix came, I was ready.

The mist grew thick and the feeling I was being watched shivered down my spine. I snapped my head up and blinked away my fear. I searched the mist, until slowly a portion of it thinned, and the head of a woman emerged from the water.

My breath caught at the raw beauty of the nix, for what I could remember in the grotto was more shadow than form. Her dark hair floated around her like a living creature as her skin shimmered an angry red. My own anger spiked, and I didn't wait for her to speak. I grabbed my wet skirts and stood, wading out toward her. "Give him back," I yelled.

My aggression made her blink. She held up her hand. "Stay where you are, human, or risk your own death."

The forceful command stopped me cold. What had she done to Ryne? Had she come to tell me he was gone? Water swirled around my thighs as tears coursed down my cheeks. "Where is he? Give him back. Please. I beg of you."

"I cannot."

"Why? He has done nothing to you."

"But he has. His fair face has stolen my heart as I

have stolen his. He does not wish to return to you."

She understood her affect on men, and over the ages she had played her charms to their fullest. I did not see how any man could resist her. A tiny fissure ripped into my faith. Had Ryne fallen victim to her as well?

Ryne loves you.

With a certainty I couldn't explain, I knew the strange voice in my head spoke the truth. I narrowed my eyes and spat, "You lie."

Her skin suddenly changed to a dusty rose and she waded closer. Her dark hair instantly dried and covered her body in long shining locks. "Look at me. Listen to my voice. What man would wish to leave my side? None. All love me. *He* loves me. He is mine. Forever and always."

She then opened her palm to reveal the handkerchief I'd given Ryne. "He bade me give this to you as proof." She unfolded the cloth to reveal a small treasure. "Take it and leave us be."

The roll of the tide rang in my ears. My mouth opened on a deep, shaky breath. I stared at the embroidered cloth that labeled it mine, at the small ransom of jewels, disbelieving what I saw. My heart gave a painful squeeze. Ryne would never willingly relinquish the token of my affection. Nor would he try to buy his freedom. What had she done to him?

She twisted the cloth together and held it out. I lifted my hand toward the handkerchief. "Ryne?"

She suddenly tossed the cloth toward me and disappeared. The handkerchief landed in the water near where I stood, and I immediately stooped to find it.

Gordie came up behind me and tried to lift me up, but I fought free until my fingers closed around the handkerchief. "Where do you go? Into the lake?" he asked, wrapping his arms around my waist and hauling me out of the water. "Do you wish to die, too? Please, Nari, you cannot do this to yourself. To us. He is gone."

I glanced over my shoulder, toward the empty lake. "No. She was here. The nix. She was here. Ryne's alive."

Once on land he let go and slanted a doubtful look at me. "If she was here, what did she say?"

I showed him the cloth, unwrapped it and poured the sparkling gems into his hand. The large, sapphire blue stone settled on top. As Gordon eyed the treasure, I traced my fingertip over the simple design I'd embroidered, unable to believe Ryne had willingly given it back. "She claims he doesn't love me anymore."

Gordie scratched at his ear, clearly hesitant to speak. "Nari. What makes you think she's telling the truth? The nix has killed every man who ever dared the lake. He's most likely dead."

"What of these?" I asked, pointing to the gems. "Did I just find them in the surf? She told me he lives. I know it to be true. You have to believe me. Ryne *is* alive." I'd grown so agitated, I nearly screamed my belief in his face.

Gordie rubbed my back and nodded as if he were humoring a crazy woman. "Calm down. You are going to make yourself ill again."

I shrugged off his hand and shoved my fingers through my hair. I could easily pull it out from frustration. "I am heartsick, Gordie. I know the truth, yet no one believes me and their distrust stings worse than nettles. I have not lost my senses. I know I am the only one who believes he is alive. I cannot explain why I do, for when I try, I sound demented. I just *know* it to be true"

Gordie nodded, his usual jovial face a mask of seriousness. "Then I believe you. But there is another aspect you have yet to consider. I think, if all the stories are true, a man is incapable of resisting a nix. And if that is so, there is nothing you can do. He is not coming back."

"Do not dare say such a thing." I shook my head, unwilling to believe him. "She is keeping him prisoner."

"Nari," his voice still held a note of doubt.

I felt sick inside. Did no one believe me? I turned my back on him, clutching the handkerchief to my chest as I sank to the wet sand. "The nix is a fool if she thinks I will accept her word. Ryne loves me. I know he does."

Gordie squatted beside me, his face pointed in the same direction as mine, and he sighed. "Sitting here, staring out at the lake and starving yourself won't make him come back."

"What else can I do but wait?"

"You have never waited for anything in your life, Nari. Why would you now?"

I turned to him and studied his profile. Was this a trick? Was he just humoring me to get me home? "What do you mean?"

"If you really saw the nix, and you believe Ryne is alive, find a way to get him back."

"How?"

He shrugged his broad shoulders. "Maybe someone in the village knows more about the nix than we do. Maybe they've heard other tales…other myths that may sound more real to us now."

My heart jumped a beat; it was almost too painful to hope. "Maybe…"

He held out his hand. I stared at it for a long moment, indecision warring inside, until I finally placed my hand in his. He smiled. "If there is a way to get Ryne back, we'll find it."

"You believe me, then?"

He looked at the handkerchief in my hand. "I don't know. It's all so strange, isn't it? But you've never lied before, and Ryne is my friend...so..."

I hugged him, and pressed a grateful kiss to his cheek. "Thank you, Gordie."

What had I expected? A change of heart? Bravery? The villagers were halfwits. And as they lounged in the warm pub, ale in fists, I told them so.

Gordie pulled me aside, wary of the disgruntled looks shooting our way, and whispered for my ears alone, "Insulting them is hardly the way to win their favor."

Anger had taken hold of me, and I was sick to death of the lot of them. "What do you suggest?" I was running out of ideas.

"Tactful logic."

I cast a glance at the people. They were half drunk, and getting drunker by the second. Slurred murmurings came from half of them, light snores from others and an enhanced cheeriness tickled the rest. They were here to drink their worries away, not to hear about my 'fanciful ideas' as some had called them.

I didn't hold out much hope, but I went to the least glassy-eyed man and appealed to any remaining compassion lurking within his soul. "What if it were you? Would you not wish for salvation?"

He snorted and muttered into his cup, "My father never fished on that lake."

"Mine either," piped up the man next to him. "Everyone knows it's cursed. Course I'd begun to have my doubts, but no longer."

A chorus of agreement rose.

I shot a glance at Gordie. He shook his head, and then nodded toward a back table where Douglas and Cyril huddled over their ales. I pushed my way to them, and saw them shrink when I did. I would not be put off. "What of you, Douglas? He is your friend."

"Was my friend," he corrected.

Douglas had always been selfish and mean-spirited. I turned my attention to Cyril. He had a sweeter nature. "Think of the good times we had. How Ryne befriended you. Does that not mean something?"

Cyril cast a watery gaze up at me, silent and afraid, but one searing whisper from Douglas turned his gaze away.

I stepped back, horrified by their rejection and glanced around the room. These were people who had known Ryne all his life. Knew his family. Had been their friends. Disgust coloring my words. "So this is how it is to be? You sit here in comfort while Ryne is held captive?"

They all muttered to one another until one finally spoke up. "His fate was sealed the day he were born. He's gone. Drowned by the nix. We've nothing to do now but wait for the body to float up."

A collective nod followed, and as the publican gathered a crop of empty mugs, he shot a quick glance my way. "It's been a bad day for us all. You'd do well to follow their lead. Forget about him. Sit down and have a drink. No one will blame you."

I reared back as if I'd been bitten by a rabid dog. "Never. I will not rest until he is found." My breathing grew harsh. "I pity you all, for to be so cowardly is a bitter legacy." I ran out the door, angry tears spilling down my cheeks. I dashed them away, determined not to let their callous behavior affect me.

Cowardly, indifferent scoundrels, every last one of them.

"Nari," Gordie called after me. "Wait."

I tripped over my own feet and would have fallen if it weren't for old man Tiller. He appeared out of nowhere and clamped his hand over my mouth, then yanked me into the alley. I struggled against him as Gordie ran by. And after a moment, he pulled his hand from my mouth.

"Mr. Tiller," I gasped, shocked at his manhandling and the hidden strength in his wiry old arms.

He quickly let go. "Sorry I am about that, but I couldn't help overhearing." He nodded toward the pub. "Was just about to go in and I thought to meself, 'Self, you needs to help that girl.'"

As old as dirt, with one lame leg and a mind gone numb long ago by too much ale, I hadn't the foggiest idea what he could do. Mayhap he was working on a plan to get even with me for all the pranks Ryne and I had played on him when we were children. I truly regretted spitting on him. Should I say so? His mind was so riddled with holes, did he even remember?

I took a step back, eyeing my retreat. "Thank you. You're too kind, but…"

He snaked his hand out and clasped my arm, keeping me from darting away. "Always fidgeting, you are. Come here." He waved his gnarled hand and a challenge glittered from his eyes. "I've got the answer to your problem, if you've a mind and the courage to hear it."

That stopped me in my tracks. I looked at old man Tiller with a newfound appreciation. He wasn't just old, he was positively ancient, and the crazy stories he told…well maybe they weren't so crazy. Surely he knew more about the nix than anyone.

"Courage? I have plenty of that."

He threw me a lopsided smile. "Good. To fight a nix, you'll need magic, and I know where to get some."

17

Sage Hill

Magic? I hoped old man Tiller wasn't playing me for a dimwit. Certainly, I deserved a healthy dose of retaliation, but must it be now? A cruel trick indeed. But with his hand waving frantically at me and his old rheumy eyes swollen and blinking like an owl's, I was desperate enough to listen to him–I had no one left to turn to. I stepped closer.

His sour breath reached my nose as his words reached my ear. "Go to the sage."

I leaned back and coughed lightly, rubbing my nose for good measure. "I've never heard mention of a sage or magic."

He barked out a laugh. "For good reason." He leaned even closer, and it took all my willpower not to pull away. "People don't trust her. But it's said she's a wise, powerful woman, and I fear she's your only hope now."

Of course, there had to be a wise woman. All tales had one of those. He was deep in his drink, and I was wasting time standing here listening to his rambling. I wriggled my arm free. "Well then. I thank you for the tip."

"Where do you go?" He sounded angry, and the last thing I needed was an old, lame, angry drunk chasing me down the street.

"To find the sage."

"Phisha," he spat and grabbed hold of my arm, again. "Don't be daft. You don't know where to look. No one listens to me. I told him to stay away from the lake. That evil lived there...but he don't listen. I could've told him about the way her skin changed colors and the way her hair whips around her...but nay. He wouldn't hear none of that. Nobody listens to me."

This old man had seen the nix? Suddenly he was far from crazy. I quickly changed my attitude. "You're right. I'm a silly girl."

"That be the truth."

He needn't be so ready to agree. I bit my tongue and smiled encouragingly. "How do I find the sage?"

An arthritic finger, bent and swollen, pointed to the East. "Go to the far hills, and make your way to the one covered in stones and briars."

I turned to stare at the eastern hills, easily spotting the one he mentioned squatting inhospitably amidst its forest-covered sisters. He had to be joking. No one traveled to that hill. It was a nasty lump. A wart on an otherwise perfect landscape. I cast him a quick glance, but he didn't look like he was joking. I pointed toward the hill, just to make sure. "That hill? Are you sure it's that one?"

"The very one. She lives at its top."

Worry fell over me. "But it's over a day's journey."

"Sounds about right."

"How does anyone reach her?"

He glanced at the hill and scratched his head. "Well, you walk for some distance, and then you climb."

"Through briars and over jagged rocks?" Why did all the wise people of lore live in such terrible conditions? If they were so wise, wouldn't they find a gentler place to live?

"If she don't like you, that's the least of your problems. Well," he said, letting go and nudging me out of the alley, "you best get to it if you have a mind to save poor Ryne."

I watched him step and drag his way to the pub door. Before he went in, I called out a soft, "Thank you."

He peered back at me and put his bent finger to his lips. "Remember, I didn't tell you nothing."

Even he recognized the craziness of his advice. I stared at the closed door, not knowing what to do. Everyone had given up. Even Ryne's parents. Since the moment their son was taken, they had gone into mourning, not even trying to save him.

Crazy old man Tiller. Could I trust him?

My gaze rose to the hills beyond and to the one covered in briars and rocks. It was too ridiculous to believe. A magic sage. But hadn't the nix seemed just as unreal?

What if it were true?

I couldn't take the chance it wasn't. I would do anything to save Ryne. The sage was my last hope.

A day later, I stood at the base of the most hazardous hill and looked up. No path. Rocks and briars tangled against each other in a wall of terrible proportions. How was I to climb through all this? Frustration nearly made me want to weep. To come all this way and find an impenetrable mess was too much. A hummingbird darted forward, hovered in front of me, and then zipped into the brambles as if to encourage me forward.

It was a good omen. I followed, climbing over a series of jagged rocks whose rough surface scratched my legs. Once over, I was met by a clump of twisted branches covered in thorns. The bird lit high in the brambles and looked down at me.

"Do I go through here?" I asked.

The bird fluttered its shimmering blue feathers, but I couldn't tell if that was a yes or a no. I pushed against the thorny outcrop and snapped off a clump at its base. Before I could take a step forward, the briar quickly grew back.

Unable to trust what I was seeing, I snapped off the newly grown section. Again it grew back.

I tore at the brambles, but as fast as I snapped off a branch, new growth appeared. I tried pushing my way through, but the thorns lashed out at me, ripping into my dress and puncturing the skin of my hands. With a cry of pain, I yanked back.

As I rubbed my stinging flesh, I watched the briar leisurely repair itself as if declaring its triumph. Finally, I collapsed on the rocks, my clothes torn to pieces and my skin raw. I picked up a small stone and threw it into the bushes. "Why won't you let me in?"

I shot a frustrated glance at the bird. "So tell me, how am I to proceed?"

The bird only fluttered its wings and turned its back on me.

It looked insulted, as if were being rude trying to

force my way up the hill. Of course. Standing, I gazed far up toward the top of the hill. "I need your help," I shouted. "Please."

I glanced down one side of the bramble wall and then the other, praying a section would magically open. Nothing happened. No sign of help or that anyone but the hummingbird could hear me.

Tears hovered at the edge of my lashes. "I would never disturb you, except love has made me bold. I will stop at nothing to bring him back to me. No evil will stop me. I swear to that. But I cannot do it alone. You are my only hope. Please, help me."

The air hung heavy with silence and then a sudden, stiff wind shook the brambles and suddenly the briars pulled away like a door swinging open, and the rocks flattened into a smooth pathway. The hummingbird cheerfully darted through and I followed, hefting the torn pieces of my clothes out of the way as I ran up the path. It wound around rocks and bushes, the bird urging me higher and higher, until finally I reached the top of the hill where a house made of brambles and rock had been built. In front, an old woman sat in a chair crushing a cluster of pungent leaves with pestle and mortar.

With gray hair piled on her head and a shawl hanging from her thin shoulders, the sage looked like a gentle grandmother waiting for her grandchildren. She bent, revealing a swallow nesting near her braided bun, and accepted a clump of mint leaves from a mouse as if it were the most natural thing to do. Straightening, she stared over at me, her silvery eyes fathomless. The coarse wool shawl slipped off her shoulders and the swallow flew down and pulled it up before settling back in the woman's hair.

I didn't know what I'd expected, but this frail, little

woman with her tiny helpers wasn't it. I hesitated, not knowing the rules that governed visiting those that held wisdom.

"You nearly drowned," the sage finally said, lifting her gray gaze toward me.

"Excuse me?" What was she talking about?

"When you saw he was no longer in the pool. You thought to end your life."

I furrowed my brow, remembering how easily it would have been to die. "How do you know?"

"I know a lot of things. More of some things that I shouldn't, and less of other things that I should. But this. I have been waiting for this moment for a long time. As soon as she took him, I knew."

A strange little smile tipped her lips. "The nix would have been pleased if you had died. I am glad you listened to me."

"What do you mean?"

"I told you he was alive. You doubted for a moment. Thought you were crazy. But now you know. He is alive. And *you* must find him."

"That was you?" She was the voice that had penetrated my misery? If that were so... "Then you knew I was coming?"

She nodded.

I looked down at my torn clothes and scraped flesh. "Then why…"

"Love is never easy."

"If you know all about me, then you know why I've come."

Again, she nodded. "What do you wish of me?"

"Help me save Ryne from the nix. No one believes he's alive but me. I am the only one who is willing to save him before it's too late."

She sat working the pestle against the mortar. Pound and twist. Pound and twist. The vein of her thought was covered by the rhythmic action. I had come for help, but she could easily turn me away. What if the deed were impossible? What if I was not strong enough? What if my journey here had been a useless cause and Ryne were already dead?

The last thought spiked fear through me. I fell on my knees before her. "Please. Tell me I'm not too late. Tell me he is still alive."

Her hand stilled and her eyes bore into mine. "Do you want me to tell you what you wish to hear, or do you wish to know the truth?

My body tensed. I couldn't live another moment in ignorance. "The truth."

"So be it." The old woman closed her eyes and began to hum.

A crisp wind whipped through the hilltop, causing the small swallow to duck its head within the gray tresses. The mouse squeaked and ran away, and I hunkered down, my breath suddenly puncturing the air with puffy white clouds as I shivered at her feet. When the woman opened her eyes they were as white as a snow-capped mountain.

The nix is bound deep within the lake,
though soon her binds will loosen.
Woe is that day, the day of her freedom,
For death will quickly follow.

Her eyelids fluttered down against her suddenly pale skin. The wind settled, and the mouse slowly came out of its hiding place. A shiver raced down the sage's back, and when she again opened her eyes, their unnatural whiteness was gone, replaced by sadness. "He is in more danger than ever."

"How can I help him?"

"Let's have some tea."

"Tea? Are you going to read the leaves?" I had heard how some wise women did that.

"Not at all, dear," she said slowly rising from her chair. "I always get a chill after a vision. Come along."

She hobbled into the house, and I rose to my feet and followed her.

The kettle was already on and the water hot. She emptied the crushed tea leaves mixed with mint into two mugs that were waiting on the table. "Do you mind pouring?" she asked. "I have something for you."

I stood in the doorway, my gaze wandering to encompass the whole room and finding it a homey mesh of nature and needs. And just like outside, tiny creatures were making themselves busy. A collection of mice darted in and out of an overturned boot, reattaching a new sole to the leather. I jumped to the side as a squirrel skittered past with a bunch of herbs in its mouth and watched it climb the wall and hang the bunch from the rafters to dry. On the far side of the room a goose nudged a ball of yarn into a basket while a fox pumped the pedal of a spinning wheel as a raccoon fed the wool.

No one would believe me if I relayed the sight. Not even old man Tiller, and he believed almost everything. I could only stare, dumbfounded at them all, and as I stared, their work slowed until they were all looking at me.

The heat of embarrassment crept up my neck, and I executed a quick curtsey, and stuttered painfully, "E-excuse me. S-she wants me to pour."

Why I expected one of them to start talking, I couldn't explain, but when it was clear none would, I stepped over to the fire, bunched my skirts together to buffer my skin against the kettle's hot handle and lifted it from the fire. As I poured the water, I heard the sage rummaging in another room. The animals had resumed their work by the time I finished pouring, and I put the kettle back on its hook. Straightening, I wiped my hands on my skirts, turned and gasped. The old woman stood directly in front of me. An intensity shone from her that caused the hair on my neck to rise.

"Never trust a nix."

The advice was given much like a scolding. I nodded. "And never shall I."

"Good." She went to the table and placed the basket she carried on top. "We haven't much time, so we must work quickly. We need to outwit her. Give her a reason to come near you."

"We want her to come near me?" That didn't sound particularly promising. "But she threatened to kill me."

The sage shot a steely glance in my direction. "Do you love him?"

"Yes." There was no hesitation. I loved Ryne more than anyone.

"Then you must risk much, even death to rescue him."

I stared into those hard eyes and nodded. "I will do whatever it takes to free him."

She dug out a large shell and held it out to me. "Take this. When you leave here, go directly to the edge of the lake. Night will have fallen. Blow into it until a mournful tune sounds. As soon as you do, the mist will rise, and she will come. The nix must obey the summons. She has no choice."

I took the shell and frowned. "But you said she was bound—"

"She will soon be free." The agitation in her voice quickly silenced me.

This," she said, pulling out a necklace made of brilliant colored stones, "is what you will show her." She grabbed my free hand and placed the necklace in the center of my palm. The stones had been polished smooth and felt warm to the touch.

"Do not give it to her. It is your lure. Whatever you do, stay out of the water and away from her reach. She cannot harm you if you are on dry land, for a nix is a creature of the lake and only the lake. Whatever is done. Whatever is said. Do *not* trust the nix."

She took both gifts and wrapped them in some cloth and packed them in a leather pouch along with a small loaf of bread, a wedge of goat cheese and a bottle of tea. Her worried gaze lifted to mine. "I have a horse that will take you back, but you must go now. You must reach the lake by midnight, for that is when she will be free."

She ushered me through the house and out the door to where a pure white stallion stood. On seeing us, he shook his mane and stamped his hooves as if he were eager to be off. She slung the pouch over the horse's back and gave me a boost. Sitting astride the animal, I tangled my fingers in the heavy mane and looked down at her. "Thank you. I—"

"Do not thank me yet, for I fear…" She dropped her gaze unable to finish. Giving my leg a gentle pat and squeeze, her face vacillated with a show of grief.

My chest tightened, and my breathing grew shallow. If she believed my mission a hopeless endeavor, then what chance did I have?

Suddenly, a firm resolve appeared on her face. Her eyes sharpened as she stared up at me. "We must not lose heart. Tell the nix she must bring Ryne to you. It is your only hope of stealing him from the nix. Do not compromise. She must bring him to the surface. Only you can do this. No one else."

"And if she doesn't bring him, what then?"

"She will, for she will do anything, *brave* anything, to have the necklace. What happens after he appears, I cannot say. But I have faith you will know what to do."

18

The Nix Knows Naught

*H*urry. The word flew on the wind, rolling over me and the stallion, urging us faster and faster. Noonday turned into evening and evening into dusk. I leaned over the horse's neck and gripped his mane tighter as he raced forward, his breathing deep, his legs strong. We darted through deep woods and charged through ripening fields. The ground we covered amazed me. Night closed in and overtook us, but the stallion still did not falter. Exhausted, I could only cling to his back and pray.

The darkest point of night hovered in the air as the stallion burst through the woods and onto the shore of the lake near where Ryne's house stood. Sand and rock flew in the air as he jolted to a stop, his lungs heaving, his legs shaking. I slid to the ground and collapsed. Never had I been on such a harrowing journey. The horse neighed and flung his head, his body quivered, drawing my attention to the pouch. This was no time to give into weakness. I had only moments before the nix would be free. I had to call the nix now or I may never see Ryne again. I forced myself to my feet and pulled the pouch off his back. As I tipped the bag and shook the contents onto the sand, the horse went to the lake and took a long drink.

The moon's silvery light illuminated the shell. I wrapped my right hand around it, my fingers perfectly fitting along its boney spine while my left hand slipped against its smooth interior. Coming to my feet, I drew a deep breath, put the shell to my lips and blew. Just as the sage had said, a mournful sound emitted from the shell.

I slowly lowered it, and stared out over the lake, searching for even a whisper of movement. My fingers ached against the shell's spines as the minutes passed. Too many minutes. Was one call enough? Should I sound it again? I didn't know.

From the corner of my eye, I saw the horse bolt away from the water. My senses sharpened. I stepped forward, my gaze intent on the horizon. A line of mist had formed and was barreling over the water toward me.

I'd never seen it form so quickly or move so fast. As I stared wide-eyed with amazement, it rushed ashore, slamming into my body so hard, it knocked me off my feet. The shell landed in the sand, but I didn't bother retrieving it. The nix was coming. I needed the necklace, but I couldn't see. The mist was so thick, I could only hear the water's rhythmic lap at the shore. On hands and knees, I crawled, patting the sand, my fingers outstretched and shaking. Idiot that I am. Why didn't I retrieve it first? She would be here any moment.

My fingers splashed against water. Was it a puddle or was I too close to the lake? The hair on my arms rose.

I didn't know, but I felt a presence. I turned my head and froze. The mist thinned to reveal bare legs wrapped in coal blue skin standing in the shallows before me. The nix's face was wreathed in anger, and her hair whipped around her like dancing black flames.

"How dare you call," her voice rumbled threateningly and she came to the edge of the lake. "Who gave you the shell?"

I scampered back, the warning to stay out of her reach screaming in my head. As I did, my hand touched something smooth. I slanted my gaze downward and saw the necklace lying half buried in the sand. Relief eased the tightness in my chest, but only for a moment. I was not safe.

Casting a worried glance at the nix, I slowly gathered the necklace into my fist. "I wish to make a trade."

The nix leaned forward, It was evident she wanted nothing more than to attack me. "He is mine. There will never be a trade."

She turned and began to wade back into the lake. If I didn't act now, she would be gone. I swallowed with difficulty and raised my hand, letting the necklace unravel and hang from my fingers. "Even for this?" I yelled after her.

"Nothing can tempt me," she shot over her shoulder.

I stood and took a step forward. "I think you are wrong. You *want* this."

The confidence in my voice must have intrigued her, for she stopped, turned ever-so-slightly and glanced back. Her eyes locked onto the necklace and her face instantly hardened. Her skin flashed red to purple then back to the deep coal blue. The look on her face made my blood run cold.

"Where did you get that?"

My heart was beating frantically, but I would not let her see my fear. "It doesn't matter. You want it. I have it."

"It is not yours to keep."

My own anger rose and I sneered, "Neither is Ryne, but that has not stopped you."

The water exploded before her, creating a shallow path while the excess waves surged around me, wetting my hem and seeping through my shoes. I panicked, and stumbled back as she charged forward. My back slammed up against a tree, the bark digging into my arms. The horse whinnied somewhere in the distance, and the nix's face loomed before me, her hand clawing toward the necklace. I screamed and dove behind the tree, falling into a ball as I curled myself around the necklace.

I had to keep hold of the necklace.

She mustn't get the necklace.

My breathing sounded ragged to my ears as I waited for the nix's hands to rip me apart and tear the necklace free. But no harm came. The wind died, and the water sounded far away. Slowly, I uncurled my limbs, got to my feet and peered around the tree. The water had returned to its tide and the nix stood in the surf with her back toward me.

I eased around the tree, stepped onto the sand and inched my way closer.

"What do you want?" Her voice sounded sad, resigned even.

"To see Ryne."

She turned and it was then I noticed her skin had changed into a dusty rose, the color highlighted her beauty in a way no other color did. "Come," she said as she waded a few feet into the lake.

I instinctively stepped forward, but caught myself. The nix didn't seem to notice as she bent, dipped her finger into the water and twirled it until a small whirlpool formed. She glanced up at me. "Come and see. Look. He is safe. Unharmed."

My feet moved on their own. To see Ryne safe. To know he was alive…

Never trust a nix.

I suddenly stopped. "No." I shook my head. "Bring him here. To me. I want to see him, to know without a doubt that he…"

I couldn't say it. I would not allow myself to believe he preferred the nix to me. My voice grew stronger. "Bring him here."

The nix's color paled. The whirlpool vanished and her skin flashed violet. She waded backward, staring heatedly at me. "Tomorrow night."

I nodded stiffly, and she threw her arms over her head and arched into the lake and out of sight.

My legs gave out, and I collapsed onto the soft sand. I'd done it. I'd made a deal with the nix and she would bring Ryne to me. I slipped the necklace about my neck, curled into a protective ball and fell into an exhausted sleep.

When I awoke, I found myself on a bed and in a cottage I knew very well. Ryne's mother sat in a nearby chair sewing as she hummed to herself.

I eased myself up on one elbow, a feeling of panic rising. "How long have I been asleep?"

"Most of the day." She looked over at me and smiled.

The room was dark. Only one candle gave off light, and it sputtered near Ryne's mother. I glanced toward the window as I pushed the blanket off me. "What time is it?"

The sun was just saying its final good-byes for the day, coloring the waters of the lake a bright orange. Ryne's mother knotted a thread. "You have time."

"What do you mean?"

"I could not sleep last night. Since Ryne…well, I cannot find peace. When I went outside, I saw you. I saw her. I heard everything. Nari, you were so brave."

I didn't know what to say. I stood and realized I wore only my corset and shift. A quick glanced confirmed Ryne's mother was repairing my torn dress. The necklace. My hand immediately went to my neck and to the string of stones lying there. I sighed in relief.

"For once," Ryne's mother said in a contented voice with no trace of sadness, "I am glad you were such a hellion as a child."

I frowned, not understanding what she was talking about. "You are?"

"Yes." She bit off the thread along the top of the sleeve and stood, shaking out the creases in my dress. As if this were a common occurrence, she rose and held the dress out for me, and with twinkling eyes said, "I have no doubt that if anyone can save my son, it is you."

19

Mine

The sun had gone to bed and the moon had begun its nightly climb as I wolfed down a bowl of stew. Between mopping up the bits and pieces with a thick slice of bread, I relayed my recent adventure to Ryne's parents. When I was done, the air crackled with tension.

His father sat in the chair before the fire and suddenly smacked his palms on his knees and shot to his feet, shaking his head. "This isn't right. I should be the one risking my life. Not some slip of a girl."

I threw him a wary glance. "This is no longer your fight. This is about me and Ryne. The sage made that very clear."

"Surely, as a grown man—"

"We know the fight is in you," she said softly, "but Nari is right. This is no longer our fight. If it were, the sage would have made it known."

He harrumphed, and stared into the fire. "Maybe.

Maybe not. How wise is a woman to send a girl to do a man's job?"

I stood and approached him. "You cannot interfere. We cannot risk it. Please. I know what I am doing."

A slash of doubt crossed his face. "Do you know that she has killed dozens of men whose only crime was to fish in her lake in order to feed their families? In my pride, I ignored the legend, placing it in the realm of superstition. I dared the curse. *I* caused all this. And now you want me to stand back and watch that evil creature wreck further havoc? How can I?"

The tortured look on his face pained me. "You must. It is the only way. Do not fear I go unprepared. I have given thought to a plan." I didn't know what else to say.

He grabbed my hands and peered down at me. "You don't understand. Just thinking of you getting harmed scares me."

And to think many in the village had scoffed at this man for years. He had far more goodness in him than any of the other men. I squeezed his fingers. "It scares me, too. But living without Ryne scares me more. Do not try and talk me out of this. It is for me to see him home, and only me."

Ryne's mother came up beside us and took off her shawl. "Take this, and tell us what more we can do."

"Other than finding me some rope? I need you to stay away," I said, accepting the shawl she held out to me. I looked at them both pleadingly. "I don't know what she will do if she sees either of you. We cannot risk it."

Ryne's mother slipped her hand into her husband's, drawing his gaze. "She's right."

With a sigh, he hung his head and gave a reluctant nod.

I rose up on tiptoes and kissed his brow. "All will be well."

When the mist rose, I would be on the shore, waiting for Ryne to come home. Nothing would stop me from making that a reality.

Never trust a nix.

The horizon lay clear before me. Midnight had come and gone. I let my hand wander to the shell which I'd found not too far from the remaining crumbs of the loaf and partially pecked wedge of cheese the sage had given me. I drummed my fingertips against it, debating if I should call the nix or continue to wait? The temptation caused my fingers to wrap around the shell, but at the last moment, I pulled away. I had to wait. She would come. She wanted the necklace more than Ryne. *She would come.*

I built a small fire to chase away the chill of night and sat beside its cheery flames. I wondered how Ryne had survived this long in the nix's world. What magic had she cast to keep him alive? And why would she want to keep him out of all the men she had captured? It didn't make sense. Had she truly fallen in love with him? Goosebumps rose along my arms at the thought. To be loved by a nix would be a frightening thing.

The flames grew smaller as the moon began its descent and the night neared its darkest hour before dawn. I stood and paced. What if my aim was off? What if the nix ripped the rope from my hands? I bit my lip. Worry tore at my confidence. I fixed my gaze on the horizon and any change it brought. And then, in a blink of an eye, the mist bubbled from the water, growing larger and thicker with each breath I took. I quickly removed the necklace and twined it within my fingers, the rocks resting easily between my knuckles, then grabbed the rope and hid it behind my back. When the mist rushed ashore, my nerves tingled like a spring coiled too snug, and I tightened my grip on the rope as I waited for the nix to appear.

Within moments, the water gurgled and the head of a man crested the lake's surface twenty feet off shore.

I squinted, trying to peer through the thickening mist. "Ryne."

I stepped forward, right to the edge of the water, and then stopped. Why was he just hovering there? Why did he not come to me? A chill crept over my heart. I quickly tossed out the rope, and it landed only inches from him. "Ryne, grab the rope," I shouted.

He looked at me, but said nothing. Did nothing. "What is wrong? Tell me?" I willed him to move, to take the rope, but instead he slowly sank beneath the surface of the lake and vanished.

"Ryne," I screamed his name over and over again. Tremors seized my body. The rope fell from my fingers. I wrapped my arms around me, wishing they were his. I stood at the water's edge and willed him back, and just when I thought my heart would break, the nix appeared.

She rose from the water, her hair instantly drying into silken waves that curled round her. She cast a sad look at me. "So you see, he is well. He wishes nothing to do with you or your world. He has returned to mine and will stay there forever."

I stood rooted to the spot. I was in shock. Despair ran like ice in my veins. Though my mind warned of my danger, that I was too close to the water, I couldn't move. The nix walked right up to me and stopped.

"Poor human," she cooed.

I saw her move. I saw her lift her hand, but my body refused to stir. Her gaze followed her hand as she stroked my cheek with the tips of her fingers, the touch gentle, yet chilling. "His love for you is gone."

As suddenly as my paralysis came on, it disappeared, and I knew. Whoever that man had been, it hadn't been Ryne. *Never trust a nix.* With great delight, I pulled back my arm and slammed my stone-wrapped fist into her jaw, spinning her to her knees.

"He. Is. Mine." I spat the words into her stunned face.

There was no question, I was in trouble now. I quickly went to the fire, pulled out a branch with one end spitting flames, and spun to face the nix. I advanced on her, brandishing my weapon before me. "You have proved nothing, and the necklace is mine until I hear from his own lips he does not love me."

As the nix stood, clouds darkened the sky and the wind whipped the water higher. My once flaming torch sputtered and died. The tide rose, and the nix slowly advanced. "Know this. When I am through with you, you will beg for death."

I would die. My heart yearned for Ryne to know I had done all I could to save him. And then a noise sounded behind me. Ryne's father stepped forward. He held a spear in one hand and a net in the other. "Leave her be," he boomed into the rising wind.

The nix stilled, and even backed up when he jabbed the spear forward and swung the net as if to catch her.

"Give me the necklace," the nix wailed, even as she moved back.

"Bring Ryne back," I demanded.

"Never. Trust is something I can no longer afford."

I held up the necklace so she could see it, ignoring

the waves crashing closer and closer. "If you want this, there is only one way to get it."

The nix stared at the string of stones the wind whipped against my hand.

"It's your move, nix," Ryne's father said.

The nix swung to face him and hissed. Without warning, a gust of wind stirred the sand into a swirling funnel. He threw his hands up to protect his eyes and the nix snatched the net from him and flung it high into the air where the funnel whisked it out of sight. Ryne's father grabbed my hand and tried to pull me behind him.

The energy the nix was using to sustain her magic was taking a toll on her. The color of her skin had begun to fade and her beauty held an evil slant to it. I should have been terrified, but all I could think of was Ryne.

I yanked my hand free and stepped forward, holding out the necklace like a wriggling worm on a hook. "Let Ryne speak for himself, and I will give you the necklace willingly. I promise."

Her gaze returned to the necklace and greedily watching it. I could see her weighing her options. With Ryne's father so close and the spear tightly held in his hand, and dawn only moments away, there was little she could do. Her gaze snapped to mine. "You have proven yourself as deceitful as the others. I will not bring him here. Tomorrow night when the moon is at its zenith, I will take you to him."

She was giving me an option that had little risk for her and a great deal for me. How she would manage the feat, I could not fathom. All that mattered was that she would take me to Ryne. We would be together, and together we could win.

I nodded. "I shall be here, Nix."

Her eyes flared with triumph, and as soon as the nix

dove into the lake, the wind stilled and the water calmed, and the first rays of dawn broke through the dark clouds and sliced through the mist, cutting it to shreds until it was no more.

An intense wooziness settled over me, and I shot a glance at Ryne's father. He stood tense, disquiet draining the color from his face. "God save us, Nari. What have you done?"

The sky spun, my knees gave way, and he jumped forward and caught me in his arms. Ryne's mother burst through the trees, her face a mask of fright, just as a large goat and cart ambled forward from the opposite direction, the sage snapping heavily at the reins. They all converged on the same spot and stared at each other before looking back at me.

"Well," the voice of the sage stabbed at the air. "That was not what I'd hoped for, and everything I feared."

20

True Love

Ryne's father carried me to the cart and settled me on the seat with the help of his wife. The sage pressed a cup of her cool mint tea in my hands while she threw an anxious glance at the calm waters of the lake. "A deceptive calm. I feel her anger burn."

She hopped out of the cart, walking stick in hand and went to her bag tied to the short bed behind the seat. With a tiny grunt, she hefted the bag closer. The heavy thunk the bag made as it scrapped along the planks caused me to jerk and the tea I held to slosh on my skirts. With shaking hands, I put the cup down. I was a physical wreck. My nerves stretched to their limit. I felt ill prepared to deal with anyone let alone the sage. But there was no avoiding her. When I looked back, the sage held a severe eye on me.

An uncomfortable silence fell. I shifted against her stare and looked away. Why was she here? What had I done to curry her disfavor?

Her eyes narrowed on me. "Never trust a nix."

So that was it. She thought I'd disregarded her advice. I had not, though that didn't stop a measure of guilt from riddling my mind. "I know."

And I did. But if I erred, it was not done as a deliberate act of defiance. "My only thoughts were of Ryne."

The sage frowned harder. "She has every intention of killing you."

"I know."

"I do not think you do."

The sage went to a downed tree and sat, her small frame tottering upon the huge trunk. She gripped the top of her walking stick and leaned forward, her gaze intense. "A nix's feelings are too elemental, too naïve, if you like. She wants, therefore she takes. Her life is that simple. The true nature of a nix was never intended to be harsh. What she understands of evil is a shallow mimicry of what man has taught her, but it is always lethal."

Alarm rippled across Ryne's father's face. "Finally some sense. Nari cannot meet with the nix tomorrow. She does not understand the risk." He turned toward me. "I have already lost a son. Must my mistake harm you as well?"

I jumped to my feet, fearful he would somehow stop me. "I have to go. If there is even a slight chance I can save Ryne, I will take it."

"You heard the sage, Nari," he said. "You can't trust the nix. She *will* kill you."

I climbed out of the cart and faced him, my back straight, my mind made up. "Then I die, but it will be a death worth risking. Ryne would do the same if the nix held me prisoner."

"Of course he would, but he's—"

"A man?" the sage sniffed. "Do not belittle Nari's

path because she is a woman. You are wrong. She knows the risks."

"Do you?" Ryne's mother stepped close and swept my hair from my face. Sorrow flowed from her very core. "You know I want him back too, but what I just saw, the fierceness of that creature. If you died…"

I'd grown my entire life without the tender caress of a mother, and her honest show of affection nearly undid me. I bit my lip and forced the feelings away. I would not let Ryne down. "It is my choice to make."

"Then it's settled." The sage jumped to the ground and returned to her bag. With a great deal of digging, she pulled out a dagger, its blade long and dark. "Soon after you left, I had another vision. I saw you beneath the water, facing the nix. A turn of events I did not foresee before you left. Because of it, I have brought you two more gifts. One has an obvious purpose," she said and held out the dagger. I accepted it, though I was revolted by its filth. Its weight lay thick in my fingers and the darkness covering the blade appeared to be…

"Is that blood?" To my horror, it still looked fresh. A shiver of disgust ran through me.

She retrieved it from me and placed it on the seat where I'd been sitting. "My magic has preserved the blood of the only thing that can pierce the nix's heart."

I waited for her to tell me more, but instead she touched the golden belt she wore around her waist. It immediately slipped loose, like a thick coil of living, molten gold, lengthening in her hand until it looked like a rope. "And this. A gift you will need, but one I hesitate to give to you. The magic it holds is extremely unusual."

Fascinated, I made to touch it, but the sage pulled back.

"The rope will do whatever the owner tells it to do.

But there is a catch. You must keep it with you at all times. Wear it as a necklace, or a bracelet. A belt such as I. It will accept whatever job you give it. But once you break the bond of ownership, it will never obey you again. You can only break contact with it for the most dire reason, and then for only a short time."

She stared deeply into my eyes. "You say you love Ryne more than your own life."

"I do," I hurried to assure her.

She closed her eyes and scrunched up her nose. Her face wrinkled with concentration. A faint chill rushed in, but it soon dissipated. Her lids flew open, and her gaze softened with dismay. "I wish I could see into his soul, but I cannot. The nix's magic interferes with mine." She glanced at the golden rope. "There is a degree of anxiety, a great hesitance on my part…"

The gray in her eyes deepened with uncertainty. "Nari. Does Ryne love you?"

I opened my mouth to reply, but she held up her hand. "You must be sure of your answer. Something tells me it is of the utmost importance. If he has fallen under the nix's spell, you could be trapped in the lake forever. Make no mistake. You risk your life by what you are about to do. Are you sure his love is true love?"

Nothing would ever make me believe Ryne would willingly choose to stay with the nix. I knew he loved me. All the significant moments—good and bad—in our shared life whipped through my head. The constant thread we shared grew stronger, knitting a picture of our past, present and future together in a way that could not be denied. We were meant for each other.

I refused to let anyone rip that joy away. I slipped my hand in my pocket and wrapped my fingers around the handkerchief. The nix had brought me the cloth, had told me Ryne did not wish to leave her, but it was not true. I stood before the concerned gaze of the sage and said in an unwavering voice that rang loud and clear, "He loves me as I love him."

"Then hold out your hand."

I did, and she let the rope slowly coil into my palm as she recited something in an ancient language. When she said the last word, she let the end of the rope drop and I felt a nip of energy rush through my hand. I glanced at her, and she sighed. "Let us hope you can find its use before it's too late."

I slipped my fingers around the golden coil, feeling a warm glow flow through my fingers as I did. Its smoothness calmed me; its crafted perfection thrilled me. I thought it would make a pretty bracelet, and it suddenly slipped along my wrist and wrapped it in a thick loop. Not one flaw could be seen along its shining length.

"It's beautiful, but how can such a little thing help me?"

"I am not sure. I have given you what I can. My visions show me that the nix will take you deep into the lake. But that is all I know. Wherever she has taken Ryne is not a simple place one can walk out of. If it were, I think we are all in agreement, he would be here now."

The sage picked up the blade from the seat and placed it in my hand. "You must kill her, Nari. It will not be easy. Harm may find you. Do not give up. You must strike the nix's heart with this blade. Only the heart and only with this dagger. Then, and only then, will you be free."

Ryne's father stepped forward and shook his head. "This is madness. There must be another way. Her anger stems from me. I should go."

"No." The sage's compassion was tempered by the

harshness of her words. "In your ignorance, you laid the fight at your son's feet, and through his love, it was passed to Nari. There is nothing we can do now but pray."

Night fell, and the moon began its climb. Its half sliver valiantly poured light down on the lake and the sandy shore. I retucked one of Ryne's cloaks closer. The feel of the soft, well-worn fabric from a pair of his old trews and shirt comforted me, though they hardly warded off the descending chill. I came to the break in the forest where the shore met the woods and huddled in the shadows, cautiously surveying the area. All was quiet. Too quiet. The sage had refused me any company, even Ryne's father, who had blustered at her plan and who insisted he follow.

"This is Nari's journey," she had reiterated to us all.

So here I stood. Alone.

My limbs quivered as I stepped beyond the trees. "I am doing this for Ryne," I told myself. But the wait, the not knowing what to expect or how I would deal with it…it was that which was tearing a hole in my confidence. I brought my fingers to the smooth, stone necklace encircling my throat. "For Ryne."

I glanced up at the moon. How such a beautiful night could hold a storehouse of impending misery was unfathomable. It was a night for lovers. For soft kisses and whispered promises. I thought of all the tender moments Ryne and I had shared, and I desperately wanted more. I would risk all for more. My very life.

If my fear caused me to refuse this journey, my love for Ryne would keep me here, staring out over the lake, forever a sad, lonely woman. I shuddered at the thought. When the nix came, I would do whatever she asked. I would not leave my love in her hands a moment longer.

The half crescent slipped higher and higher, and higher still until it hung over the lake, spreading its soft glow from shore to shore. The time was nigh. Expectation surged through my veins. The reflection of the night stars danced on the water's surface...and then, just along the horizon, the mist appeared. It grew thick, billowing along the surface toward me like a wall of liquid silver. When it came ashore, it hit me with a mighty force, causing me to stumble back a few feet. The mist rose higher, springing around me as it enveloped my body in a world of white. Its heaviness dampened the sound of the lake lapping at the shore even as my vision grew cloudy. My lungs expanded as I fought for air, but only found vapor. I clutched my throat. Was it possible to drown while on dry land?

I coughed and sputtered. My eyes watered, adding to my misery. The wall of pure vapor pushed past me and I found myself in a pocket of lighter mist. As I blinked to clear my vision, a large, unfamiliar shadow rose. It was not the nix, but something more powerful and far more terrifying to behold. I couldn't believe what I was seeing. Dragons weren't real. But here one materialized seemingly out of nowhere, a creature just as mythical as the nix and far more threatening. Waves rose against the huge body as it slid soundlessly through the water. I staggered back, my mouth agape, my heart frozen in my chest. I couldn't scream. I couldn't run. I could only stare in disbelief at the monster rising from the mist. The dragon's massive triangular head towered over the lake, and when it dipped its head, its horns jabbed at the mist, causing the heavy vapor to spin and roll off their evil points.

It came right up to my face, its breath a hot sulfur, its scales a shiny purplish-green reflection of the water. My fingers grazed the hilt of the dagger hidden in my trews, the thin blade hardly adequate to kill such a beast.

The large head tilted from side-to-side so its yellow eyes could examine me. I felt insignificant—a morsel not worthy of its interest, yet here it was, sizing me up for its next meal. As we continued to stare at each other, the whirl of fear I felt slowly faded. We stood nose-to-nose for a moment and then the beast lowered its head, resting it on the sand, and opened its jaws.

A long rumble came from deep within the dragon, a gentle sound almost like a purr. My mind refused to register what I knew it wanted. I stared past the rows of sharp, jagged teeth and into the pitch blackness of its throat.

"She cannot be serious," I said on a shaky breath.

I was to enter the dragon? It was a prospect that paralyzed me. I couldn't. No sane person would do such a thing. My fingers brushed against the necklace at my throat, feeling the smooth stones, and I realized the full extent of my dilemma. If I did not enter the dragon, Ryne was lost to me forever. But if I entered the dragon, I would most assuredly die.

The dragon stirred and moved ever-so-slightly forward as if to urge me inside its gaping jaws.

I had no choice. If I could manage to stay in the mouth, I had a chance of survival. But how? As my mind searched for an answer, I felt a strange movement along my arm. I glanced down and saw the golden bracelet grow. It slithered into my hand and lengthened into a whip thin rope.

That was it. With shaking fingers, I grasped a

pointed tooth, secured the rope between it and the tooth next to it, and gingerly climbed inside. The tongue felt spongy under my feet. I tried not to think of where I was or what a reckless thing I was doing. This was the only way to Ryne.

As soon as I was completely inside the mouth, the dragon's jaws snapped shut. Without me even saying a thing, the rope twirled around my arm, clinging to me as much as I clung to it. My racing heart gave one frantic beat before the dragon spun around and flew into the air.

My feet flew out from under me and the rope lengthened as I dangled freely in the darkness, live bait for the taking. I could feel an intense heat swirling near my feet. I unclasped my cloak and let it fall, hearing it flutter downward. In a shock of light, it suddenly burst into flames and for the briefest moment, I saw my surroundings. The tongue writhed, flicking at the rope in an effort to loosen its grip and spur my body toward the back of the throat. I tightened my hold, grabbed the knife and jabbed at the tongue. It lashed back at me, knocking me to and fro. I cried out, and the golden rope bit harder into my arm.

Suddenly the dragon rolled into a dive. I tumbled toward the jagged front teeth, but before I hit, I was quickly thrown back toward the yawning gullet again. The force of the dive pulled at my skin and shuddered through my body. When we slammed into the water, a heavy spray rushed into the dragon's mouth, soaking me.

The force that had kept me toward the back of the throat immediately abated, and I slammed against a row of front teeth. Their jagged edges cut into my skin and caused a bump to swell on my head. The arm on which the rope had tightly coiled itself ached along with my shoulder. The smoldering heat that had been walled far down the throat slowly crept closer. I began to sweat. My lungs burned from the rising temperature and the infusion of sulfur.

Eaten or slowly roasted alive. My future did not look promising. The darkness was oppressive. The stench overpowering. I felt sick. My head began to spin. But then the heat and sulfur smell suddenly lessened and in the next moment, the jaws opened and a wall of water rushed into the mouth. I gasped my last breath of life before being overtaken by the flood. I used the rope to pull myself out of the dragon's mouth. A dim sliver of light outline the body of the nix. The rope released its hold on the teeth, winding itself around my arm the moment the nix seized my hand and tugged me forward. I was quickly towed out of the nightmare I had placed myself in and into a watery tunnel.

The minerals in the rocks mirrored back light. My lungs, already bruised by the journey and poisoned by the sulfur, screamed for fresh air. When I saw the light grow brighter, I yanked my hand from the nix and bolted forward. I crested the surface of the pool and was greeted by a cavern and Ryne, huddled in the corner, bare-chested and shackled to the wall. Though his legs were free, his hands were cruelly manacled together in front of him.

He looked at me as if he were seeing a ghost. Weighted down by chains and exhaustion, he struggled to his feet, and staggered forward. "Nari?"

21

It's Over

Ryne tripped over the chains and fell to his knees, but his attention was still solely focused on me. "Get out," he rasped.

He wanted me to leave? But I'd just found him.

"Get out of the water. Now."

His gaze shot over my head. Horror leaped into his eyes. I glanced behind me and into the angry face of the nix. Panic flooded my blood. I floundered back, but when I turned to swim away, the nix had zipped behind me, forcing me to come up short. I could feel her angry breath, see the hard, unforgiving glint in her eyes.

A deadly smile creased her dusty rose-colored face. Slowly, as if a watercolorist used a broad brush, midnight blue lines crept over her skin, spreading out until her whole body flushed darkly. A malevolent laugh burst from her throat. "You are a *fool.*"

She suddenly sank in the water, instantly blending with its darkness. Ryne's hoarse warning sounded right before I was yanked under.

The water rushed over me too quickly, and the air I managed to take soon grew useless as I hit the bottom of the cave's pool. I pushed at the bottom and began to rise toward the surface, hitting at anything that threatened my safety. But I fought a shadow. Her skin was so dark, she blended in with her surroundings. I popped to the surface, took a quick breath and was yanked under again. She attacked before I could find my bearings. Toying with me, she darted here and there, attacking, then retreating. Several more times she allowed me to gain the surface, but each reprieve was just long enough to gasp a lungful of air before she pulled me under again.

It felt as if she had six grasping, hurtful hands. Her nails, sharp and biting, darted toward the necklace. Each time I managed to fend her off. Her anger heated the water and her intent switched from grabbing the necklace to inflicting as much pain on me as she could. The sting of each cut delivered along my arms and legs made me jerk away. I fought toward the surface, sputtering when I reached the top. Ryne's yelling collided with the roar of panic flooding my ears.

I was weakening. I had to get out of the water. I was in the nix's element, her domain. Her place of power. She would win if I couldn't reach dry land. I whipped my legs into a frenzied churn, and raked my arms through the water, terror driving me toward the cavern's shelf. I had to get out. Now.

Suddenly, my head arched back as the nix grabbed my hair and yanked me under. I twisted around and grabbed hold of her arms. Face-to-face, I saw the hate radiating from her glowing eyes. If only I could stop her from attacking me. Somehow hold her still.

The unsaid desire caused the golden rope to slither down my arm and wind around the nix's torso, clamping her arms to her body. The nix let go of me and struggled against the bright coil, but the rope only tightened its grip. Free, and with the nix bound, I rose toward the surface, praying the rope would hold. When I crested the water, I climbed awkwardly onto the shelf.

My chest felt heavy, each breath an ache as I dragged in as much air as I could. Water cascaded from my fingertips, rolling down my body to the uneven ground. Ryne knelt motionless before me, shock rippled over his beloved features. But not for long.

"Nari." Ryne regained his feet and struggled forward; his gaze would not leave the water. "Where is she?"

I glanced behind me, not really sure, just grateful to get away. "I-I don't know."

He thrust the heavy cuffs forward. "Hurry. Set me free."

I rushed forward, my hands shaking when I touched his face. "I thought I would never see you again."

I placed a kiss on his mouth, but he pulled away, his voice abrasive, "There is no time."

His gaze was still latched onto the water and a deep foreboding shone from his face. I clasped the cuffs that kept his hands imprisoned together, feeling the jagged iron bite into my hands. Muscles straining, I tore the pin out and ripped the manacle off his right wrist. He sucked in a painful gasp as it fell away, but immediately turned his attention to the other manacle now that one of his hands was free.

As he worked, his face bore a deep, disturbing paleness I hadn't noticed before. Multiple slashes of dried blood flaked against the cuts on his skin, while purple bruises flared under the silvery moonlight. I cupped his cheek. "What you must have suffered."

He cursed at the rusted iron and glanced over at me. "You should not have come. If she harms you..."

I put my finger to his lips. "I do not care. I am with you and that is all that matters. Here. Let me try."

I grasped the other manacle and forced the corroded pin out, and just as the cuff popped open, a noise unlike any I'd ever heard rumbled through the cavern. We both turned toward the water. The surface began to bubble and steam, and the water became incandescent. Dead fish floated to the surface. The mica embedded in the rocks glowed brightly as something orange gurgled upward.

Ryne suddenly grabbed me and threw me to the ground. He curled his body around me, shielding me as the fire burst from the water and leapt toward us. I could hear the flames sizzle against the water, smell the scorching of cloth and feel the rock around us heat up. The skeleton chained lopsided to the opposite wall burst into flame, the old, dried clothing and leathery skin a perfect torch. Sulfur coated my throat and stung my eyes. I knew that smell and that bitter taste. The nix was loose and she had commanded the dragon to burn us alive.

The flames flickered close, arching over our heads to blacken the walls and ceiling. The fire raged for so long I feared my lungs would turn to dust if I drew one more breath. But then the flames receded, and I pulled away, coughing and gagging, miraculously unharmed.

Ryne moaned, rolled off me and staggered to his feet. Facing the water, he rasped tensely, "She's coming."

I glanced at Ryne, fearing the worst, but his skin held only the faintest trace of pink, not a blister or scorch mark marred him. The fire had risen far above us and the heat had only singed the tips of his hair.

He became a man possessed. Grabbing the base of the chains, he tugged, but the peg embedded in the wall held tight. "Help me get this out."

I grabbed a portion of the chain and pulled. Nothing happened. Not even a slight nudge. With a growl of frustration, Ryne pushed me away and lifted the chains. He ran his fingers along the links until he found what he was looking for. His arms bulged as he tried to separate the weakened iron. Ever so slowly, they creaked apart until he held a large portion of the chains in his hand with the thick manacle dangling from the end.

Two specks of light slithered in the water.

He pushed me behind him. "Get back."

I flattened myself against the rocks as he hefted the chain above his head, and swung it in a tight, fast circle. The manacle clattered as it flew, like an angry, snapping jaw waiting for its prey.

His chest labored for breath. He had grown weak from lack of food and little rest. He grimaced as he concentrated on the nix slithering toward us.

When she finally surfaced, his face grew taut, and his eyes hard. With a sudden explosion of energy, he threw himself toward her and let the manacle zip downward.

Water flew forward to intercept the manacle, and a massive wave rose, lifting the nix high and dropping her on top of him. He fell to the ground sputtering like a landed fish. She grabbed his hair, twisted his head back and hit him in the chest. I thought I heard a rib crack.

She stood, a beautiful creature bent on revenge, and turned her hate-filled eyes on me, but my eyes were only for Ryne.

I couldn't breathe. Couldn't speak. As the nix stepped away, I saw a knife—the very one I'd brought to kill the nix—protruding from Ryne's chest. I didn't need to check to see it was gone. I must have dropped it as I entered the tunnel. Why only now did I feel its absence?

Ryne's face contorted in pain; his body writhed against the agony. The nix smiled and backed further away as if to enjoy the spectacle of death.

I ran forward and fell to my knees. "Ryne. Oh God, please, no." I wrapped my fingers around the crude wooden hilt and pulled the knife free, dropping the hated thing to the ground.

He gasped. His eyes locked on mine.

"Don't die," I ordered, willing him to live. My will did not matter. His eyelids slowly fluttered shut, obliterating the life that was once in him.

"Ryne?" He couldn't be dead. A wealth of tears welled and spilt freely onto him, washing his body with grief and disbelief. He couldn't be dead. I couldn't bear to think I would never feel his arms around me or feel his lips on mine. I had just gotten my best friend back. I couldn't lose him again. "Don't go. I am here to rescue you."

In my grief, I didn't notice the nix had come up behind me until her fingers slid within my hair and twirled around a long lock. With a persistent tug, she pulled me to my feet. When I was exactly where she wanted me, she let go. I faced her, condemning the cruel senselessness of her evil. Her dark skin shone blue, then red, and then lightened to a dusty rose. "And so it finally ends. The boon is fulfilled, the bargain met. Yet what should I do with you?"

An empty deadness suddenly flattened my soul. I gave up. I would willingly hand her my own heart, anything to stop the pain of Ryne's loss.

"It doesn't matter," I rasped. I didn't care what

happened to me. Ryne was dead.

She cocked her head, and her gaze swept me. "I once loved a man."

At my silence, she smiled. "Yes. I have loved. But it was not worth the pain. You should thank me. You are better off without love."

"You are wrong. I am better off for knowing love."

She didn't acknowledge me, only hissed her evil to the rock walls. "The man I loved betrayed me. I could have given him anything his heart desired, but he turned from me."

"Maybe he saw the hate lurking within you?" I challenged.

"I never knew hate until him." She said it so quietly. Her eyes were focused far away as she returned to another time. "He killed our baby as if she were an animal, and then he hunted me. They all did. From that day forward, man called me monster."

"And you proved them right."

Her eyes snapped to mine, the remembrance of long ago shuddered behind them once again. "It is too late to free you now. The die is cast. Your soul shall wander these waters with the rest of them."

I stood tall, unafraid of anything this creature would do. I let a confident smile touch my lips. "I will be in good company, then."

"You are brave, but still a fool."

A movement caught the corner of my eye. The nix must have seen it too for she turned, and a snarl of outrage fell on her beautiful face. Her anger roused my alarm. I fell back just as Ryne lunged forward and plunged the dagger into her heart.

The nix cried out. Shock rocked her backwards. She clawed at the hilt protruding from her chest, astonishment shattering her perfect features. Her gaze rose to mine. Confusion mingled with fear. "How can this be? I am the nix. I have always been."

I didn't know what to say. I turned my face away as she lay down, unable to watch her die as she had so many others. I heard the clatter of the dagger as it hit the ground, yet when I looked back, she clutched the knife to her chest. The glow of her eyes faded. "He has finally killed me. My beloved's blade, the one of my child's doom, has found me."

The light behind her eyes that pierced the darkness of the deepest waters grew dim and died. Her skin cracked, and she withered into a pile of bones. Only her hair lay thickly round her. Like a dark silk veil, it cradled her body.

My limbs began to shake and I collapsed to the ground. I pressed my fingers to my mouth, unsure why a scream fought to be free.

Ryne knelt before me and reached out his hand, but I reared back. The shock of seeing him alive was almost too great. "H-how can you be alive? I saw you die."

"It is a miracle. One brought on by your tears." He showed me the area where the knife had been, but not even the slightest scratch could be seen. His whole body looked perfect. Completely healed.

I touched the area, felt the warmth of his skin and burst into tears anew.

"Nari." My name fell softly from his lips. He slipped his hand against my cheek and whisked away the falling tears with his thumb.

His gentleness was my undoing. I threw myself against his chest. I wouldn't believe he was real until I felt his arms around me. And when he cradled me close, I finally let myself breath. The nightmare was over. Ryne and I were both alive.

"We did it, Nari. We are free. Forever. No longer will I fear the lake. No man will." He kissed my cheek and spoke of his love…but my gaze fell on the nix. She lay at rest on the ground, but not at peace.

I pushed away from Ryne, a sudden urge consuming me. "She said something about a child. Her child. It died. Murdered, I think."

Ryne stilled. "I found a tiny skeleton."

I bit my lip, knowing he wouldn't understand, but I felt the need to heal this one wrong done to the nix. "Will you help me do something?"

"Anything."

He brought out the tiny skeleton swaddled tightly in faded green linen and tucked her within the crook of the nix's arms. I unhooked the necklace from around my throat and placed it atop the pair of them, then backed away.

"She is at rest now." I glanced over at Ryne.

He touched my cheek and gave me a gentle smile. "Why do you care?"

"I'm not sure. It just felt as if she was in so much pain, she couldn't feel anything else. She was greatly wounded and could not forgive. I don't want to be like that."

Ryne stared at the nix, his gaze unfathomable. "I'm not sure I'll ever be able to forgive her. She nearly destroyed the one thing I love more than anything. You."

A gentle smile tugged at my lips. "I know you. Forgiveness will come. And soon this will all be told in rhyme and song and our children will call us fanciful."

"Will they?"

"I promise."

"Nari," he looked suddenly uncomfortable. "I don't

wish to worry you, but we're trapped."

I hadn't thought of getting out as much as getting in. "There must be a way." We'd come this far, I refused to give up now.

"There is. By water and past the dragon, which is not wise or …" He looked up and pointed. "We can climb out."

He dropped his hand and leveled a serious look at me. "I have tried the latter. It's impossible."

Impossibilities were part of our life now. Hope infused my being, and I couldn't help the secret smile that pulled at my lips. "Not if you have a magical rope."

As soon as I spoke the words, there came a scraping sound. Not long after, the golden rope inched its way from the water. I quickly picked it up and inspecting its length, stroking it like a favored pet. A few dents showed, but all-in-all, it looked sturdy.

Ryne frowned at it. "What is that?"

"A gift from a sage."

"A fine gift, but hardly practical. It is far too short for what we need."

"Do you love me?" I asked.

His eyes lit up. "More than anything."

"Then have faith, Ryne." I curled his fingers over the rope just above mine and wound his other arm firmly around my waist. I bestowed him a loving kiss, and when I pulled away, I gave him a mischievous smile. "Hold on tight."

As soon as the words left my mouth, the rope shot upward. It thinned to a mere thread and when it secured itself to the top, it pulled us gently up after it.

22

A New Beginning

The lake shone calm, bathed in the rose and magenta colors of the setting sun when Ryne pulled me away from our wedding festivities. We walked along the shore, hand–in-hand.

I'd been stealing glances at him all day. It was like I expected him to disappear and this all to be a dream. It was a pathetic insecurity, one I'd never had before. I forced myself to gaze out over the water. "I can see why your mother loves the lake. It is beautiful."

"You always liked it. You sat in that tree and stared toward the lake for hours."

"I cannot lie. I did. But the pull had just as much to do with the boy living in that pretty little house as it did the lake." I stopped and cast a quick glance at the sparkling stone house the whole village had warned his parent's not to build. "Do they regret building here?"

Ryne wrapped his arms around me, pulled my back against his chest and kissed the top of my head. "Never.

And neither shall we." He pointed toward the right. "Over there, past that small cove. That is where we shall build our home."

A house on the lake? A ripple of excitement flittered through me, but was instantly replaced by uncertainty. "Are you sure? I'll be happy wherever, just so long I am with you."

"I am a man of the water, now."

The way he said that caused me to pause. I twisted in his arms. "What do you mean?"

"I don't fear the lake anymore."

The tension I'd felt eased, and I looked out over the lake again. "A hunter, a mason, and now a fisherman. You are following in your father's footsteps, I see."

"I owe him a great deal. He was right. This whole time, he was right."

I hugged his arms closer, knowing his regret, yet feeling his love.

"Ryne," came a chorus of shouts from the people huddled around the little jewel of a house.

Amongst the crowd my father and the new wife stood. I could so easily sink into resentment and hate, for although my father never abused me, he had ignored my sorrows from the day my mother died. He had given the new wife complete control, and she had abused that power, ushering my brother and I out of their lives at every chance. But the winds of change were in the air. I could feel them touch my family. The whole village.

"Come," I heard my father call. "There are more who wish to hear the tale of the nix."

Ryne laughed and nodded. "All right, all right. Just one moment, if you please."

He turned me toward him, slipped his hands within my hair and tilted my face up to his. "Forever is a long time to be married to a myth."

"A myth no more. You are a legend. I happily give my life into your hands."

"As do I, yours," he whispered just before his lips touched mine.

Hoots and hollers rose from the crowd. And when we finally broke apart, I turned away in happy embarrassment. Ryne wandered over to the large group and sat in a chair they had pulled out for him. "Where to begin?" I heard him say.

"At the beginning," piped up a small boy.

Ryne smiled, and ruffled the hair on the little boy's head. "Once upon a time there lived a boy doomed to die…"

Thus the story began, but it ended differently than anyone could have imagined.

I married a man of legend. The nix's prize. My best friend.

And we lived happily-ever-after.

Acknowledgements

This book has been a long time in the making. It seemed no one but me ever believed in it, so it sat in a lonely file on my computer year, after year, after year, until Thursday Publishing came along. Finally, it's been made into a beautiful book. Yay!

I'd like to thank all those who made this book possible, especially the hard work and dedication of Robin Perini. She is seriously the coolest, smartest person I know.

I have to thank my family. While I am writing and editing, they are the most ignored creatures on the planet, yet they don't hold that against me and welcome me back into the light when I emerge from my cave. They are the best of me.

And finally, I'd like to thank the Brothers Grimm. Without their faery tales I wouldn't have dared to write my own.

Other Young Adult books by Shea Berkley

The Keepers of Life Trilogy (Fantasy & Adventure)
  Book One -The Marked Son
  Book Two - The Fallen Prince
  Book Three - The Rising King

Faery Tale Short Stories (Dark & Dangerous)
  Once Upon a Time: The Villains (All Six Stories)
Or buy them two at a time
  Once Upon a Time: Candy Lane/Sliver of a Soul
          (Purple Book)
  Once Upon a Time: Queen of All/Enemy Inside
          (Green Book)
  Once Upon a Time: Hag/Giant's Way
          (Red Book)

ABOUT THE AUTHOR

 Shea Berkley has a fondness for characters, whether in real life or those she makes up in her head while she's tending to a multitude of mundane tasks she's forced to do in order to survive. Writing gives her purpose (okay it keeps her out of trouble…mostly), and she can't imagine herself doing anything else.

AUTHOR'S NOTE

Thank you for reading *Mist on Water*. I hope you enjoyed it!

If you'd like to know when my next book is available, sign up for my new release e-mail list at www.SheaBerkley.com. You can also like my Facebook page at facebook.com/SheaBerkely. Don't forget to follow me on Twitter at @SheaBerkley. I'm on Goodreads at www.goodreads.com/SheaBerkley, where you can see what I'm up to and post reviews.

P.S. If you enjoyed reading this story, I would appreciate it if you would help others enjoy this book, too.

Lend it. Please share it with a friend.

Recommend it. Please help other readers find this book by recommending it to friends, readers' groups and discussion boards.

Review it. Please tell other readers why you liked this book by reviewing it.